Published in 2011 by Marplesi

ISBN 978-0-9566983-5-3

A catalogue record for this book is available from the British Library

The Good Girl

by

Sinclair Macleod

To Zoe

Lots of love

Uncle Sinclair xx

Marplesi Books

Also available by Sinclair Macleod

The Reluctant Detective

Dedication

For Dad and in memory of Mum, who taught me to love books.

As always, in memory of Calum,
my wonderful son and inspiration.

Acknowledgements

Many writers will tell you that writing a novel is a solitary pursuit that requires many people's input, I am no different.

My gratitude goes once again to Kevin Cuthbert and George Mitchell for their advice regarding police procedures and providing the inspiration for part of the story.

Thanks are also due to the staff of the mortuary in Dundee. In particular Alison Beaton and Dr Priyanjith Perera who gave me their valuable time and their knowledge of the procedures used when dealing with suspicious deaths in Scotland. I also garnered a huge amount of information on the changes that a body undergoes after death. I learned more than appears in this book and it will stand me in good stead for many books to come. I also received help from Professor Sue Black at Dundee University's Centre for Anatomy and Human Identification, for which I extend my appreciation.

My deepest gratitude is offered to Ian Morrison who supplied me with valuable insights into the workings of a vegetable farm.

Any errors that occur in these pages regarding any of these subjects will be entirely mine.

Thanks are due to Andy Melvin, who continues to edit my ramblings with skill and patience.

My love and thanks also go to my wonderful wife, Kim and amazing daughter, Kirsten. I could not do this without them.

THURSDAY 15TH APRIL, 2010

The knife slashed across my chest, slicing deeper as it crossed my pectoral muscles: the blood, a crimson waterfall, streamed down my shirt. Stone laughed as he watched me fall. His face was distorted, a rictus grin. The pupils of his eyes were completely red, an ivory skull visible through his transparent skin.

I woke with a jolt, sweat streaming from every pore. It was the first time that the nightmare had gripped me for some time. For weeks after the confrontation with Davie Stone my sleep was disturbed by the same tormenting images, memories grotesquely twisted by my unconscious mind. In the dream I had failed, Stone's knife had become my nemesis and there was no justice for Rory Kilpatrick, his mother or Mrs Capaldi. Carol had tried to persuade me to see a psychologist but I dismissed the nightmares as a passing phase. I didn't want anyone digging around in my head. I knew how much guilt was stored there and exposing it to inspection was not an option.

I thought that they had passed, those nights of sleeping terrors. I guessed they had returned with the thought of a new investigation, an unconscious connection between Stone and the new case I had taken on.

"You OK?" Carol asked sleepily.

"Just a stupid dream, I'm fine." I looked at my bedside clock, seven zero four it read in blue LED numbers: time to stir myself from our bed and start the day. I washed, shaved, dressed and filled my bag with some clothes before making breakfast for Carol and myself. Carol still in her nightwear, joined me at the dining table, dishevelled but incredibly gorgeous.

"Is it the dream with Stone again?" she asked.

"Aye," I agreed reluctantly.

"Is it this new case that's troubling you?" she asked as we tucked into the mushroom omelette I had prepared.

"I don't think so... maybe... I don't know. It's not as if this case is anything like December, it should be pretty straightforward, hopefully." I didn't know who I was trying to reassure, Carol or myself.

She sensed my unease and rested her hand on mine. A simple loving gesture that I appreciated. The discussion moved on to some inconsequential non-sense while we finished our breakfast.

Fed and filled with my first caffeine fix of the day, I was ready to go. I had already told Carol that

I would be staying with my mum in Arbroath while I investigated the new case. Before I began my journey, she gave me a lingering kiss.

"Don't be away too long."

"I don't plan to be."

She watched from the door as I walked down the stairs of the close, waving just before I disappeared from her view.

*

My new investigation had started the day before.

I arrived in the office about quarter past nine. I began by tidying away the papers that were still scattered across my desk from the previous evening.

There was little more for me to do as there had been no work from the insurance companies in the past couple of weeks and I had spent much of my spare time filing, studying policy papers and doing the boring administrative tasks that I normally avoided like it was a fifteen-year stretch in Barlinnie.

The newspapers were covering the fraud trial of New Futures Group executive Frank Maloney and I had read every word. I was relieved that the police had decided not to call me as a witness. There had been a team of specialist fraud officers investigating him since December; their evidence would be enough for the jury to contend with as it was very detailed and would take a long time to present in court. The trial was as complicated as any trial gets and was scheduled to last for four months. His role in Rory's beating had already seen him convicted but the fraud was what would put him in jail for a long time. There were multiple threads of corruption and bribery that would need to be untangled, it was not only the schools contracts that were crooked.

There was an initial flurry of coverage in the media but as the trial became bogged down in financial components, the column inches were decreasing with every passing day. The goldfish attention span of the public had moved on to more important concerns like the love life of Katie Price or the latest ridiculous creation worn by Lady Gaga.

I had filled the kettle but the office phone rang before I had even switched my computer on to catch up with my e-mail and the latest news.

"Hello, Campbell Investigations, Craig speaking. How can I help you?"

"Mr Campbell, I need your help? My friend has been missing since Saturday night. Would you be willing to help me find her?" The male speaker had a slight East European accent: the words tumbled over each other as he rushed to communicate his concerns.

"Well, give me some details and I'll see what I can do." I still wasn't sure about non-insurance work, it was still a little bit out of my comfort zone. However, at the heavily weighted suggestion of some police officers, I had obtained my Private Investigator Licence. No matter how unsure I felt, I found my return to insurance duties to be very mundane and boring compared with the challenges of finding a killer.

The caller's name was Danielus Petrauskas and he proceeded to give me a quick outline of his concerns. He was keen to tell me that he had read about what I had done in December. In the quiet period around Christmas, the story had been in the headlines for three days: my role in the affair was portrayed in the press as being rather more heroic than the harsh reality of my memories and nightmares.

His praise and belief flattered me, as he urged me to come to the Kingdom to help him. Unfortunately, he had bought into the journalists' representation of me as the hero of the hour and nothing I could say would persuade him that I was not the man he thought I was. I was acutely aware that I would let him down if I failed to live up to his inaccurate opinion of me. I was still only one man and my resources were on the small side to take on a missing persons case.

After fifteen minutes of his insistent pleading and urging, I agreed to visit him and get some more details, but I offered no guarantees that I would take the case. I told him my fees and said I would see him the following day.

*

An hour after I left Carol, I was riding along the roads of Fife, the spring sun beating on my back. The verdant vista was punctuated by splashes of sunshine-yellow rape flowers and blocks of terracotta soil: the brown fields were waiting patiently for the germination of seeds to bring them out of their winter slumber. The road was ribboned with the saffron gold of the gorse blossom, giving the coarse bushes a temporary cloak of glamour.

The open road was leading me back into the world of the detective and it was invigorating me. My concerns were being pushed to the back of my mind by the freedom of the bike and challenge of a new puzzle to solve.

In the five months that Carol and I had been together, I had spent more time inside a car than on the back of my Ducati but today was different, today I was the lone biker again: the sensation of the two wheels racing over the tarmac banished the images of the nightmare from my mind.

My destination was St Andrews, once capital of Scotland: an ancient seat of learning and the destination for pilgrims from all over Europe in the middle ages. Today, the university remained but the pilgrims came from all over the world and wore luminous shirts, loud trousers and golf spikes.

This was no pilgrimage for me, this was a new challenge, a fresh test of my skills as an investigator.

After about an hour and forty minutes of my departure from Glasgow, the "Auld Grey Toon" came into view. The Old Course Hotel stands on one side of the road like a post-modernist guardian, the brand new university buildings mirroring it on the opposite side. It is as if they are protecting the venerable, ancient, grey edifices at the town's heart from the onslaught of the 21st century.

I like St Andrews; there aren't many seaside towns in the world with the anything like the same degree of religious, educational and sporting significance. It had been a regular holiday spot for me as a youngster, summers spent on the fabulous beaches and in the attractive parks. My mum loved this part of the world so much that she had chosen to retire to Arbroath, a little way up the coast. The East Neuk of Fife had been a little out of her price range.

When you visit this ancient town, the past and the significance of the place roll down to greet you: the history of Scotland distilled into a few square miles. It is a serious town, a town of attainment, a town of sporting prowess and a town to absorb knowledge. At the same time, it is both the essence of Fife but somehow slightly apart from the modern Kingdom. It is a town of many contradictions but they all contribute to its appeal.

The temporary residents, the cosmopolitan student body, help to give it a similar atmosphere to my home in the West End of Glasgow. There are bookshops and cafés, restaurants and bars, delicatessens and expensive clothes shops. It is as if Byres Road had upped sticks and moved to overlook the chill North Sea.

I rode into town on Links Crescent, turned into City Road and then found a spot to park my bike off Market Street.

My recorder, pen and notepad tucked inside my

rucksack, I walked the short distance to Bell Street and the Gorgeous Café where I had arranged to meet my client. There was a service counter on the ground floor but the seated area was upstairs and looked more like someone's front room than a commercial location. There were a couple of traditional café tables and chairs, but the leather couches and large oak sideboard made it appear like a sophisticated apartment. The brightly painted walls were peppered with abstract paintings; a triptych of flowers and a picture of The Buddha gazed down with a serenity I could only dream of.

As it was only ten o'clock, there were no other customers occupying any of the chairs. After removing my jacket, I sat down in one of the comfortable, black leather sofas.

A woman in her thirties, wearing a white apron over her clothes, arrived to take my order. I decided on an espresso to help give me a mid-morning boost, adding to the early-morning kick-start that I had prepared for myself before I left Glasgow. Carol's attempts at getting me to switch to decaffeinated coffee had fallen on defiantly deaf ears.

The waitress disappeared back downstairs to rustle up my order as a couple of elderly women arrived and took their places at a table close to the stairs. They both looked as if they were on their way to the Kirk in their Sunday best: dressed in hats and soft leather gloves, expensive coats and smart dresses. They sat with their heads bowed over the table, talking in hushed tones, ensuring that I was unable to hear what they were saying. When the waitress reappeared they both ordered tea and scones.

Ten minutes after my coffee was delivered, a man in his early twenties appeared from the stairwell. He was about six feet tall, his build was slight, almost skinny for his height. He was wearing a midnight blue jacket, scruffy brown jeans and a black, woollen hat. His face was tanned, with a sculpted line of facial hair tracing his jaw line down to the point of his chin. His hair had avoided the worst effects of his hat, some magic gel or mousse had kept his fashionable style intact: his trendy haircut was the colour of burnt umber, his eyes were two or three shades darker. There were frown ridges on his brow as he approached me.

"Mr Campbell?" he asked tentatively.

"Please, call me Craig." I replied as I stood to shake his hand.

"Thank you for coming." As I had noticed on the phone, his English was excellent, the influence of American TV shows and movies noticeable in certain vowels.

As he removed his outer clothes I asked, "Can I get you something?"

He thought for a moment before replying, "May I have a cappuccino, please?"

I was about to walk down to the counter to give the order to a staff member when the smiling woman appeared to take my client's order.

"Can we have a cappuccino, please?"

"No problem, anything to eat?" she asked brightly.

"No, thank you." Danielus replied.

"What about you, sir?" she addressed the question to me.

"No, I'm fine thanks."

When his order arrived, we began our conversation, with Danielus occupying the chair that was at a right-angle from mine, my recorder rested between us on the small coffee table.

"So, Danielus, tell me some more about your friend."

"As I said on the telephone, my friend Ah-leets-ya has disappeared. I hope you can find her."

"How do you spell that?" I asked

"A; L; I; C; J; A" he replied and I noted it in my pad.

"Maybe you should tell me what has happened, from the beginning." I suggested.

"I work with Alicja at the Rose Farm, about five kilometres from here. We work together as general farm help, picking vegetables mainly. I have been in Scotland since September 2008, Alicja arrived in February of this year. We are friends since then."

I nodded as I began to take notes.

"Alicja went to a party in town last Saturday, she did not come back to the farm after the party had finished. I am worried that something bad has happened to her."

"Are you and Alicja a couple?"

A shy smile crossed his face before he replied, "No, we are just friends. I am gay, Mr Campbell, Alicja does not interest me in that way. I came to Scotland to work as it is easier to be like me here, there is more tolerance, I think. Do you understand?"

"I think I do. What makes you think that Alicja might be in trouble?"

"She is a good girl, she always phones her mother in Poland once a week, every Sunday without fail. Her mother did not get a call this week. Alicja's clothes and other personal things are still at the farm, she has not been in contact with anyone at home."

"Does Alicja have friends or family in Scotland that she could possibly be visiting or even living with?"

"Her friend, Stefania, came with her from Poland and I think the rest of her friends are at the farm. She may know other people but I'm not sure if they are friends."

"Have you contacted the police or the hospitals? In case she's been in an accident."

"Yes, but there is no report of anyone like her in the hospitals. The police say there is little they can do, she is an adult and many adults go missing every day. They say they do not have the resources to find her. How can that be, Craig? How can people mean so little? Is it because she is a migrant worker?" There was a tinge of both disappointment and anger in his voice.

I tried to reassure him. "No, I'm afraid that what the police have told you is correct. There are many people who decide that they want to start a new life. They abandon everything they know for a fresh start, leaving their friends and family. Some never get in touch again, others find their way home after a while. It is difficult for the police if there is no evidence of anything suspicious happening to her, she is an adult."

"Alicja would not need a fresh start, she was working here to help her family back home in Poland. I know she would not walk away from her responsibilities, she is very good to her family." He was firm and positive in his answer.

"Do you know where in Poland she comes from?"

"Grobice, I think it is a few kilometres south of Warsaw."

"Have you contacted anyone in Poland?"

"No, but Stefania has spoken to Alicja's mama, she is very worried."

"I can imagine. What about the authorities there? Is there any record of her arriving back?"

"She does have her passport with her at all times, we all do, it is easier when you are far from home. I have not spoken to anyone in Poland but I called the Polish consulate in Edinburgh two days ago. She has not been in contact with them either."

"OK, is there anywhere else she may have gone, a local boyfriend, maybe?"

He shrugged. "If she has one, she did not tell me but she was very private about these kind of things."

"If you don't mind me asking, Danielus, why are you doing this? It is a lot of money to spend to find a friend, no matter how close you are."

He looked up, a serious expression on his face. "When I was fourteen my sister died, she was only sixteen. It was a cancer that took her from me. My family was devastated, my father did not cope at all. I still carry the pain with me everywhere, it runs deep in my soul. I love Alicja as a friend, we have become like brother and sister in a very short time. I could not bear to lose another sister. I cannot bear the thought of the pain her mama and papa will feel if something has happened to her. Money is nothing compared with that."

"Why do you think you and she became so close?"

"She reminds me of my sister, her sense of fun, her loyalty, her spirit. It is like a little of Daina has returned to me, a little of my sister travels with Alicja."

"I understand. I hope you didn't mind me asking."

His solemn eyes were blinking away tears as he shook his head. "No, it is OK."

I then decided that I should try to help him, it was obviously important to him.

"Maybe I should have a look at Alicja's room, as a starting point. It might give me some clue to what Alicja may have been thinking."

"She lives on the farm. Mr Rose rents caravans to us, they are cheap but not very attractive. I will take you." He seemed relieved to finally be taking some form of action to help his friend and that he had someone to help him.

When he finished his coffee, we gathered our belongings and I paid the bill before leaving the café.

"Do you have a car?" I asked.

"Yes, I am parked in South Street. Do you wish to come with me?"

"No, I've got my motor bike. I'll follow you. It's round off Market Street, I'll go and get it. If you stand at your car, I'll come around to where you're parked."

It took me a couple of minutes to get back to where I had left the bike and then ride the short distance to find him. He was standing beside a decrepit, dusty and dishevelled Renault Twingo. The car had Lithuanian licence plates, I think that it used to be blue but the dirt of the farm, in conjunction with the patches of rust, had rendered it a dreary shade of brown.

He was parked in front of the Oxfam shop. There was an empty spot beside him and I pulled in to it.

"We go out this way." He indicated east along South Street towards Abbey Walk. He got into the car and after a few spluttering noises from the engine and the ejection of an enormous plume of blue smoke, he reversed out of the space and joined the flow of traffic. I tucked in behind him and trailed the toxic cloud that was now belching from the car. He travelled out past the East Sands and then the Fairmont, the five-star hotel and golf resort that overlooks St Andrews Bay. After about ten minutes he indicated a turning and I tracked him up a narrow lane, over a slight hill and down towards a picturesque farmyard that lay sheltered in the bottom of a shallow valley.

He drove past the main farmyard that comprised of the farm house, a variety of barns and small equipment stores. There was a further depression behind the buildings, where he eventually came to rest. There was a group of twelve caravans organised in three rows of four. It looked like a traveller's camp had parked up in the field behind the farm buildings.

Someone had erected a flagpole at one edge of the camp. Flags fluttered from it, the colours of Poland, Lithuania and Ghana joined by the Saltire and a few I didn't recognise. It was the little bit of decoration that added some life to the miserable scene.

I dismounted the bike and followed Danielus towards a run-down, pale green static caravan in the first row. The shell was stained with a sinister green moss, the tyres below the main structure were nearly flat. His home seemed to rest precariously on concrete breezeblocks and was held down by steel cables fixed to spikes in the ground. There was a desolate air to the place that seemed depressing, not a place you would look forward to returning to after a day of strenuous physical work.

Danielus opened the door. "This is the home I share with George. He is from Ghana," he added by way of an answer to a question that I hadn't asked.

I followed him into a dark, dingy, narrow space with a low ceiling. The smell of spicy food fused with the aroma of creeping damp permeated the air. It was chilly despite the spring warmth outside, as if the sun's rays never quite reached the interior. Inside this mobile residence it was always winter.

"It is not much but it is my home for now." He smiled but seemed embarrassed.

The door was in the centre of the caravan, to the left was a minuscule kitchen and beyond that an equally cramped living area. On the right there was a short corridor that I presumed led to the bedrooms.

"Please take a seat." He moved some foreign language newspapers that were lying on the couch in the living space.

I sat down while he fussed around tidying away the papers and emptying a small bin that sat below a wooden unit. A portable television occupied the space on top of the cupboard. There were pictures of an African family pinned to the wall, happy children laughing at the camera with the joie de vivre that adults seldom replicate. The bright clothes of the kids gave some cheer to the melancholy atmosphere. There were no photographs of Danielus or his family anywhere to be seen.

"I will take you to see Alicja's trailer in one moment." He passed from sight along the corridor. There was a great deal of door banging, the sound of drawers being opened and closed, the caravan rocking gently and squeaking in accompaniment to the movement. When he returned he was dressed in overalls and a high-visibility vest.

"I have to work when we are finished or Mr Rose will be unhappy with me."

"That's OK, I don't think it will take long. I need to have a look around and see if there is anything that might give me an idea of where to start looking for Alicja."

He finished dressing in the living room by pulling on a pair of safety boots over his thick grey socks.

When he was fully equipped to face his working day, we stepped back out into the spring light. My eyes struggled to adjust to the brightness.

Alicja's caravan was in the middle right of the four, in the same row as the home that Danielus and George shared. We walked the short distance and Danielus opened the unlocked door.

In a design that was almost the mirror of the Lithuanian's home, there was a lighter feel but it was still very confined and slightly claustrophobic. The air was more fragrant; an air freshener competed with a cheap perfume for the attention of my nose.

"Are the caravans always unlocked?" I asked.

"During the day we normally leave them, there is

no one else to come here, except the workers."

"Is there another girl who shares with Alicja?"

"Her friend, Stefania."

"And she'll be out working at the moment?"

"Yes, we are picking carrots and cutting cabbage this week. Do you wish to see Alicja's room now?"

"Yes, please."

He preceded me as far as the door to Alicja's room and swung it open for me. I stepped into the compartment but there was not enough floor space to allow him to join me. It was decorated in regulation beige, with faded flower-patterned curtains hanging limply at the window. The bed was smaller than a standard single: although it was about the same length, it was about two-thirds as wide. A bright pink duvet cover gave the room a splash of attractive colour and character, two small cuddly toys sat in sentinel positions on top of the pillow. On the meagre bedside table were a pair of glasses and a Polish language novel: a historical romance judging by the picture of the couple in 18th-century clothing on the cover. At the end of the bed was the thinnest wardrobe I had ever seen. I manoeuvred into position around the edge of the bed, closing the room door to allow me to open the wardrobe. I was amazed at how many clothes Alicja had managed to pack into such a small space. There were some T-shirts, jeans and a single dress. On the floor were a pair of pink summer sandals and high stiletto heels in a vivid shade of turquoise.

I opened the room door again to talk to Danielus. "Where are her working clothes?"

"She keeps them under the bed." He pantomimed a lifting motion to show me how to see the space under the bed.

I did as I was instructed and sure enough there were some working clothes folded in neat piles. I was about to put the bed back down when a book caught my eye. It was at the pillow end of the pallet, tucked behind some checked shirts. I reached in and pulled it out. It was an A5 notebook, bound in black faux leather. There was a strap with a pop button holding it closed. I opened it to find pages filled with neat, feminine handwriting. It was all written in Polish but seemed to be a journal or a diary from what little I could gather.

"Did you know that she kept a journal?"

For the first time Danielus seemed to be puzzled by my English. "Journal?"

"A diary, a notebook of what she did each day?"

"No. I was not aware of this." He was now confused for a different reason, as if wondering why anyone would do such a thing.

"I don't suppose you can read Polish."

He replied apologetically, "No, I am sorry, I cannot."

"Do you mind if I take this with me?"

"No, if it will help find Alicja, please take it."

"I'll bring it back as I might need Stefania to

translate for me if I can't find another way."

"Yes, I'm sure she could do that."

I finished in the bedroom and walked behind my host to the living room.

"Are you finished now?"

"Just a couple of questions."

"Yes." He looked as eager as a puppy waiting for a ball. He was obviously keen to find his friend.

"Do you have a photograph of Alicja I could take with me?"

He turned and looked around at a small cupboard in the galley kitchen. There was a series of pictures on the door of two girls in their early twenties. He picked one of them and handed it to me.

On the left was a very attractive young woman with brown hair, highlighted in tones ranging from the colour of melted caramel to the pale hue of toasted oats. Her eyes were green with a fleck of hazel, shining from behind the spectacles I had spotted on the bedroom table. She was dressed for summer, her skin glowing with seasonal colour. She looked happy and carefree, the way young people should look when the sun shines.

Her friend had plainer features, a round face, topped with hair dyed a rich shade of scarlet. Her fair skin was covered in freckles, ice blue eyes were separated by a button nose. The overall effect was like a child's doll rather than the young adult she obviously was. The one exception to her childish appearance was a row of pierced earrings that decorated her left ear and gave her an aggressive edge.

"The girl on the left is Alicja, Stefania is on the right." Danielus pointed to each as he spoke.

"That's great, are you sure it will be OK to keep this?" I asked.

""Yes, I will tell Stefania you have it."

We stepped out into the farm yard again, the sun was now hidden by some gloomy clouds. The air suddenly didn't seem quite as welcoming; the chill dying breath of the long hard winter before it succumbed completely to the advances of spring.

"Danielus, I'm sorry to be talking about this but we'll have to come to some financial arrangement." I always found asking people for money an uncomfortable and embarrassing moment. It was much easier to send an invoice to a faceless administrative clerk in an insurance company.

"I'm sorry Mr. Campbell, I had forgotten. What was it you said again?" He was as flustered as I was.

"£750 advance and £200 per day plus expenses."

"I have money that I have saved that I can give you for your advance, the older Mr. Rose has agreed to help me with the rest. I will get a cheque for you now."

He went back to his caravan and returned with a cheque for the advance. As he was about to pass it to me, I heard a shout in a distinctly East Coast accent, "Ho, Lacky is that you payin' yir boyfriend fur a shag, like?"

I turned to see an obese man walking down from the main farm yard. He was dressed in blue dungarees over a thick green woollen jumper, his stomach straining like a medicine ball against the fabric. A yellow, high-visibility rainproof jacket hung from his shoulders and a checked flat cap protected his head from the elements. He was huge, at least five stone overweight, and he lumbered towards us with all the grace of a beached elephant seal.

He made a move to snatch the cheque but I had it in my grasp and in my pocket before he could reach it.

"Ooh, yir boyfriend's touchy." He made a face as if he was back in the school playground tormenting the speccy kid.

Danielus' complexion had turned a deep crimson. "Mr. Campbell is here to help find Alicja."

"That wee tart, probably away knobbin' some guy back in Polski. Wastin' yir time, ken?" The second sentence was directed at me.

"That'll be for me to decide. I'm Craig Campbell. I'm sorry, I'm not used to being spoken to in that way by someone who is too ignorant to even introduce himself. You'll need to forgive me if I think you're a prat."

He laughed but there was little humour in it, "Aw, a funny bastard. Well ye better watch yirsel'. Ye don't know who yir messin' wi'."

I yawned at his pathetic retort. "You're absolutely right, what is your name?"

"Bennett, Neil Bennett. Whit's it tae ye, like?"

I made a show of taking out my notebook and writing down his name. "Bennett. And what do you do around here?"

"Whit ye writin' ma name doon fur? Ah've goat nothin' tae dae with that wee Polack cow disappearin'." He motioned to grab the book but once again I was too nimble for him.

"Well, you would say that wouldn't you? I'll ask again, what is that you do round here?"

Like Danielus, his complexion also began to change colour but through anger rather than embarrassment.

"Ah'm the supervisor o' this useless bastard. Ah'm here tae tell him tae get back tae work. Move yir Polack arse back tae the fields, worker's playtime is over fur lazy pricks."

The need to smash the boorish clown in the face was growing stronger by the minute but I knew it would achieve nothing for either Danielus or Alicja.

"He's Lithuanian, or is the distinction too much for the peanut that rattles around your skull pretending to be a brain?"

"Disnae matter, they're aw just joab-stealin' Polacks."

"God, you really are an arse. This isn't an act." I laughed to release some of the tension I was feeling.

His proto-human brow ridges were nearly covering his eyes as he made an antagonistic move towards me.

"Neil, get back to work. You too Danielus." An elderly man commanded them from the top of the incline.

He walked down towards us as the two workers turned away: Danielus in relief, Bennett with reluctance.

"You have my number, Mr Campbell?" Danielus asked as he moved away.

"Yes. Before you go, what is the address of the flat, where Alicja went for the party?"

He stepped back towards me and gave me an address in Castle Street just off North Street. "It is shared by two students, I think."

"Thanks Danielus, I'll be in touch."

Danielus walked away with Bennett chattering away in his ear. I doubted that his words would be very complimentary or encouraging.

The elderly man offered his hand. "I'm Albert Rose, this is my farm. You must be the private investigator."

"Yes. Hello, I'm Craig Campbell." I returned his firm hand shake.

"Do you fancy a cup of tea and we can have a chat?"

"Coffee would be better."

"Coffee it is then." He led me back up to the main

farm buildings.

*

I entered the substantial, stone-built farmhouse and was immediately greeted by a pack of six dogs of varying shapes, sizes and colours. I was surrounded by a sea of lolling tongues and enthusiastic bodies, all wagging a slightly musty welcome from their shaggy tails.

"Away and lie down." Mr Rose barked the command that every animal obeyed, scurrying off to a room to the left of the hall.

Mr Rose guided me to another room on the opposite side of the hall, past a staircase that faced the main door. He showed me in to a hospitable, cosy room that looked like an old-fashioned parlour. The furniture was far from modern but obviously solid and well made. The walls were decorated in a boldly printed lilac wallpaper: a collection of ceramic plates was mounted across the main wall, a flower delicately hand-painted on each. A thick wool carpet covered the floor, its once bright colours muted to dull pastel by age. Despite the spring weather, a wood fire crackled in the hearth and offered its heat to the room, the smell of burning wood added to the welcoming atmosphere.

I removed my jacket and laid it the back of a well-upholstered armchair to the right of the fireplace. I sat in the same chair while Mr Rose worked away in the kitchen. After a couple of minutes, he walked into the room with a cafétiere of a coffee so dark it was almost black. He placed it on a small occasional table in front of the fire. He then retrieved the cups and a jug of milk from the kitchen, balanced on a wicker tray.

"Do you need sugar?" he asked as he paused at the door.

"No, that'll be fine."

As he sat in the chair opposite me he said, "I'm normally a tea man but this stuff is pretty good."

I thought I could trace a little bit of Yorkshire in his accent, which I hadn't noticed before. He was dressed in a cream-coloured checked shirt with a beige cardigan over it. A pair of rough tweed trousers covered his legs: the kind of material that looked to me as if it was the very definition of itchy and scratchy. His face was thin to the point of gaunt but his skin glowed healthily. His pale grey eyes gleamed with a hint of mischief from behind a pair of thick spectacles. His hair was receded to almost nothing and a grey moustache made him look vaguely like Bruce Forsyth.

"You're here about Alicja," he suggested.

"Yes, Danielus is very worried about her."

"Well, I'll do anything I can to help. I've told Danielus that I'll help with your costs."

"Yes, he told me. How well did you know Alicja?"

"Not very well at all. I'm pretty hands off with the farm these days, my son Colin is the manager really." He sipped on his coffee before continuing.

"Of course, I've met her. She seemed quite a quiet girl, a hard worker from what Colin tells me, but I can't say I know much more than that."

"Do you know if Colin or anyone else had a problem with her work?"

"Colin hasn't said anything if there was, but you never know. Neil Bennett would probably be the one to have problems with any of the staff, or maybe that should be the other way round." He shook his head gently as if regretting Bennett's role at the farm.

I offered my opinion. "He doesn't seem to be the best manager of people in the world, I have to say."

"I know. I wouldn't have him near the place but he was in Colin's regiment in the army. They were in the Balkans together during the conflict. Colin persuaded me to give him a job when they came out, Bennett wasn't doing too well on his own, apparently. When Colin took over running the farm, he promoted him to supervisor."

"I take it he's caused some problems with the staff?" I prompted.

"Let's say that staff turnover has gone up considerably since he stepped up. We used to have a few regular migrant workers come over every season, we've lost most of them and the ones who arrive don't seem to last too long, particularly the women."

"Have other women gone missing?"

He looked uncomfortable. "No, nothing like that. They just go home or find somewhere else to work in the UK."

"Do you think that's what Alicja has done?"

"I wouldn't know, anything's possible but from what Danielus told me she's left a lot behind if she has found somewhere else."

I pressed him. "Do you think Bennett has harassed or assaulted these women?"

He thought carefully before answering. "I'm not sure. It's possible, I suppose, but I get the feeling that he's all mouth. I suppose that would be enough to drive some people away but I can't say for sure."

I left the silence hanging in the hope he might say some more but he continued to drink his coffee pensively.

I turned the conversation to the farm. "How is the farm doing?"

"Not too badly, considering. Colin seems to have a good head for business and we've done quite well since he took over. He works all the hours God sends, never seems to sleep. We've been doing so well that we bought the neighbouring farm a couple of months ago, added quite a few extra fields. It had been vacant for about four months, a repossession apparently. You know how things have been for everyone over the past few years."

"What is it you produce?"

"Vegetables, mainly, one or two fields of cereal. Carrots and cabbage are the two main crops but the new place will let us expand into soft fruits. We should be able to sustain the business better all year round, between the two that is."

"How long have you been in Scotland?"

"We bought the farm in 1968, a few years now."

I had run out of questions and coffee. "Thanks for your help, Mr Rose. I'll be in touch to let you know how I get on." I stood and shook his hand before stepping out into the hall. As I was reaching for the door, I heard a voice call from the room the dogs had run into.

"Albert, Albert who's that?"

"It's something to do with the farm, Cath." Mr Rose pushed open the hall door into a low-lit room. I could just make out a frail, elderly woman lying on a bed.

"Bring 'im in, let me have a look at 'im." Her voice was cracked and weak, her Yorkshire tones more distinct than those of her husband, despite her time in Fife.

"Do you mind, Mr Campbell?" Mr Rose asked apologetically.

"Eh, no."

I walked into the room, the dogs lifted their heads, briefly wagged their tails and went back to lounging across each other. The curtains were closed and a dim lamp cast little light but I could see the elderly occupant's face as I approached her bed. The story of her long life was written distinctly in the wrinkles around her eyes and mouth. Her eyes were a cool green with slightly cloudy pupils. Her hair looked as if it had been spun by silkworms, thin, shining white threads of gossamer, delicately styled, probably by a visiting hairdresser. Her skin was like rice paper: my thoughts drifted back to a hospital bed in Glasgow and Mrs Capaldi. I guessed Mrs Rose to be ten years older than her husband. The tell-tale signs of life ebbing away were as obvious in her as they had been in Mrs Capaldi, even if she was going more gently.

The stale smell of a room that was rarely opened to the outside world was nearly masked by the sickly sweet perfume of a candle flickering on the mantel-piece of the fire.

She interrupted my musings, her voice barely above a whisper. "Come 'ere lad. Let's have a look at thee. My eyes aren't what they used to be."

I did as she instructed. She reached out and took my hand, provoking another memory, this time of the touch of my friend as she lay dying.

"You're a fine lookin' lad and no mistake."

"Thank you." I wasn't sure how I should respond to the situation I found myself in.

"He's a one for the lassies ye know?"

"Oh, is he?" I wondered if it was Mr Rose she was talking about or someone else.

"He was after that Peggy Cartwright but I got 'im and 'e'll not be lookin' at her again. But you've got to watch 'im all the time." She cackled a hoarse laugh.

I could sense Mr Rose moving close to my back.

"That's cos she's been dead for ten years and we haven't seen her in forty five, Cath." His voice was gentle but doleful.

"'E's got a new one now, 'e told me, came 'ere and told me, as bold as brass." She stated emphatically.

"Surely not." I said to give my mouth something to do. She was still holding my hand tightly but I was desperate to escape the couple's private world, I felt uncomfortable with her obvious confusion.

"When's Jack coming round, Albert?"

"Cath, he passed six years back."

His response didn't seem to register. "Tell him to come see me, Albert."

"Aye, pet, I will. Mr Campbell has to go now."

"Oh, that's a pity. It's nice to have visitors. Bring Peggy the next time you come." Her hand fell away from mine as if she had no energy left to hold it up.

"Can I have a drink, please Albert?"

"Will do my love. I'll just show Mr Campbell out."

"Goodbye, Mrs Rose."

I escaped the darkened room with a sense of relief.

"Sorry, Mr Campbell. She's been suffering from dementia for about ten years. Remembers everything from when we were wed but she's not so good with anything after that. Jack was her brother, he went the same way before he died. She doesn't keep too well but we keep ploddin' on."

I couldn't help but feel sorry for the poor man. He was still deeply in love with his wife and cared for her as well as he could, but there was a sense that he knew he had already lost her. She was slipping away to a world where he couldn't really reach her any more, like she was slowly drifting from the safe shore of their marriage to an island of loneliness. I hoped she would at least be happy there. I remembered the tortured paranoia of my Mum's aunt, who suffered for nearly fifteen years in a state of dejection and fear. I wouldn't wish that on either Mr or Mrs Rose.

"Right, I'll let you get on. Goodbye." I said to Mr Rose and received another firm hand shake before I walked back to the bike.

*

I rode the Ducati back to St Andrews with my mind occupied by thoughts of the task that lay ahead of me. I knew that this was going to be a test; finding someone who wants to disappear is no easy task. The mystery lay in the fact her belongings were still in the caravan but you never could tell. Maybe someone had swept her off her feet, maybe she was in a hospital somewhere having lost her memory. I would need to speak to as many of those who attended the party as I possibly could and try as many official avenues as I could think of.

Back in the town, I found the address Danielus had given me and parked the bike across the street. I rapped on the royal blue door a couple of times but there was no response. I looked at my watch and realised that it was probably the middle of the academic day. There was nothing else I could do for the moment. I decided to wait until the following day before beginning the investigation in earnest.

Back on the bike, I pointed it towards the Tay Bridge and my mother's house in Arbroath.

*

My mum threw her arms around me when she opened the door.

"What are you doing here?" a surprised grin split her face.

"Can you stand to have a lodger for a couple of nights?"

"Of course, of course. Come away in." She fussed around me, being more of a hindrance than a help.

I proffered a bag of groceries that included some decent coffee. I love my mother dearly but she's strictly a tea drinker. Her idea of coffee is instant, contains chicory and has sat in her cupboard for about five years, slowly solidifying into a single mass that requires a chisel before you can get a spoonful.

Mum's flat was the top floor of two in a row of terraced houses. The flat had two bedrooms, a living room, kitchen and bathroom. It was the ideal size for her and she had made it a comfortable home. She got on well with her neighbours who looked out for her when she needed anything, in much the same way as I had with Mrs Capaldi.

41

The spare room had a bed, a bedside cabinet and a small wardrobe. It was decorated in pink, like the majority of the flat. Mum likes pink.

I deposited my bag and bike leathers in the pink paradise and went into the living room.

"So what brings you back to your old mum? Everything's OK with Carol?" she asked.

"Carol and I are fine. I've got a case in St Andrews, I thought it would be easier to crash here, that's all."

"An insurance case?"

"No, I've been hired to find a young woman that's gone missing."

"Oh no, not that stuff again, you know what happened last time you were a detective." Her motherly disquiet showed in her eyes.

"It's OK Mum, she's probably just run off with some guy. I don't think there's any danger."

"Between that bloody bike and all the stuff that happened at Christmas, you're a worry. I know you think you're a man now but you'll always be a wee boy to me. I don't want anything to happen to you." She gripped my arm.

"I know but it'll be fine, trust me." I gave her a reassuring kiss on the cheek.

Reluctantly she agreed, "OK. Look after yourself that's all I'm saying."

"Yes, Mum." I suddenly felt like my eight-year-old self, being warned away from playing too close to the canal.

"I've got some nice mince from the butcher, how about mince, tatties and doughball?"

I was definitely back to being eight. "Sounds great, Mum."

She bustled away in the kitchen while I typed up some notes on the MacBook I had brought with me, not that there was a lot to write. I had replaced the computer that was stolen from my office with a more portable solution. It went everywhere with me when I was working.

After a hearty dinner, I called Carol and updated her on what I had found. She told me she was missing me and I confessed that I too was missing her. My mother sat opposite me with a large contented smile on her face. She liked Carol a lot and the two of them had already formed a formidable partnership designed to keep me in line and under control at all times.

Carol asked to speak to my mother and they talked away for half an hour before I got the chance to say goodbye.

I called my mate Li to let him know where I was and that I wouldn't be at the pub quiz that night. He sounded intrigued by my new case and asked to be kept informed.

The rest of that evening, I sat with Mum, watching her soaps and reality programmes on television before I went to bed around half ten, exhausted from the day's events.

I awoke from the same nightmare, the sweat drenching me again. Maybe Carol was right, maybe I needed to talk to someone, but it would have to wait until I had finished this case. I couldn't afford any distractions until I had found Alicja safe and well.

FRIDAY 16TH APRIL, 2010

I left Arbroath at eight-thirty the following morning having managed to side-step my mother's attempt to feed me a fried breakfast. A plate of fried sausage, bacon, eggs and tattie scones would have tasted magnificent but wouldn't have done anything for my arteries or my digestion.

The weather had taken a turn for the worse, frequent showers tumbled from a consistently gunmetal grey sky. The Scots word for the weather when it is like that is dreich, a sound that accurately captures the depressing effect it has on people.

I had to negotiate the Dundee rush-hour traffic, which meant it was quarter to ten before I got back to the student flat in St Andrews. I parked in almost the same spot as I had the previous day. I was hoping that the university day wouldn't have started for at least one of the occupants of the flat.

Once again I knocked on the blue door. This time I was in luck and it did swing open. Behind it was a young Sikh guy dressed in a black turban, a black vest proclaiming the name of a Goth rock band and a pair of black jeans. His muscular arms were covered in tattoos, a variety of designs vying for space. There was some Punjabi writing that I presumed was religious in origin but there were also fantasy animals: a Maori-inspired design on his left forearm and a pouncing tiger on his right.

I had obviously interrupted his daily routine as he had black eyeliner decorating his left eye while the right was only half painted.

"Hello, can I help you?" His accent was a comfortably familiar Glaswegian.

"Hi, my name is Craig Campbell. I'm a private detective." I flashed the licence card that I was required by law to carry.

"Really? Cool." He seemed impressed, not a reaction that I had received too often.

"I've been asked to look in to the disappearance of a young Polish woman, she was last seen at a party in this flat I believe."

"Well, you better come in."

The flat was really more a narrow house over two floors. He escorted me through a short hallway, past a wooden stairway into a spacious living room. Like Danielus' caravan, there were newspapers strewn across half the area. There was a pile of magazines in the corner including music; games and lifestyle titles, some clothes rested precariously on top of a chair and a general air of disorganised chaos seemed to prevail.

"Sorry, I'll clean up some of this mess." He lifted the clothes and newspapers to create enough space for me to sit down on a rickety, ramshackle purple couch. The dark patches of stains and large rents in the fabric made it look like it should be in a skip.

I sat on it and promptly began to sink, coming to rest with my knees about level with my chest.

"I'll be a minute, sorry about the couch." he muttered regretfully as he disappeared back into the hall.

While he was gone, I had a more studied look around the room. Although narrow, it was long, with the door to a galley-style kitchen to the right of the hall door. There were a couple of storage units that looked like they may have come from Ikea. There were books on biology; chemistry; mathematics; physics and engineering. The volumes lay at an array of different angles on one of the units. The other cupboard had DVDs, an iPod dock and some novels by Ian Rankin, Lee Childs and Harlan Coben among others. A large flat screen television dominated the wall close to the window, a PS3, a Nintendo Wii and a pile of games for both of the consoles lay beneath it.

When the young man returned, the decoration on his eyes was now symmetrical. He sat directly opposite me, his legs folded up beneath him, his armchair about as distressed as the sofa.

"I take it this is about Saturday's party?" he asked.

"Sorry, you didn't tell me your name."

"It's Prabihir Singh. The guys call me Hero if that's a help."

"Hero. OK. The girl I'm looking for is called Alicja. Her friends believe she attended the party." I retrieved the photograph that Danielus had given me from my rucksack and handed it over to him, pointing out Alicja as I did so.

He studied it for a short time before saying, "Yes, I do remember her. She's a bit of a looker isn't she?" He nodded as he spoke.

"Did you speak to her?"

"No, I don't think so, other than to offer her a drink maybe, but I think I remember her being with one of the guys who is friendly with my flatmate, Gerard. I'm sure they take some of the same classes. They might even have been at school together, I think."

"Do you remember his name?"

"Ralph or Rupert, something like that, posh English dude. Gerard would be able to tell you."

"Was there any trouble during the party?"

"Well, it did get a little out of hand. Someone posted the details on Facebook and we ended up with more people than we could cope with, a lot of them a bit worse for wear. It kind of spilled out onto the roof, one of the bedroom windows opens on to it. One guy walked across the rooftops of the houses in the street and couldn't get back. We needed to phone the fire brigade to come and get him down. It put a swift end to the party. The firefighters weren't too impressed, I can tell you."

"There was no fight or argument then."

He shook his head. "Naw, nothing major that I know about."

"Was there a specific reason for the party?"

"It was Gerry's 21st birthday."

"Would he have known everyone that turned up?"

He laughed. "He's not that popular, no."

"Is there anything else you can remember?"

"No, I can't think of anything that might help."

"What about Gerard, when can I talk to him?"

"I can take you to meet him at lunchtime if you want. We normally meet in the Drouthy Neebors on a Friday for a bite to eat. Do you know it?"

I remembered the name from my last visit. "It's in South Street?"

"That's right, near the old gate."

"I can meet you there. What time?"

"About half twelve."

"Right, I'll get you there." I stood up with some difficulty, feeling an ache from the origami fold in my back created by the failing settee. Not long turned thirty and the aches of old age had started already. I was relieved that Li wasn't there to see it or I would never have heard the end of it.

Hero showed me to the door and I stepped out into another squally rain shower, the wind from the

North Sea driving it hard against my face.

*

There didn't seem any point in getting on the bike again as there isn't a huge distance between any two points in the centre of St Andrews. I walked, huddled against the wind and rain. I was back in Bell Street within five minutes but this time I chose Beanscene for my caffeine fix. I knew there was Wi-Fi access there and I wanted to be able to find some telephone numbers.

Having ordered a cappuccino and a sandwich, I took my order number and the details of my Wi-Fi login to one of the tables with leather sofas at either side. I removed my own heavy bike leathers and settled down.

Across from me a student sat typing intently on a laptop, sipping his own coffee as he did so. I reckoned him to be about seventeen or eighteen, painfully thin with thick-rimmed Harry Potter-style glasses. As I watched, a young mother arrived with a little boy in a stroller. She retrieved one of the high chairs that the café offers for toddlers and put it at the table next to the student. The young man's face was a picture as he watched the child, like it was a bomb about to go off. The student flinched visibly as the child exclaimed in excitement. I doubted that he had many younger brothers or sisters, an only child possibly. It was an amusing little diversion from my task.

The young woman arrived with my coffee and food, which was as welcome as an old friend.

As it had been a couple of days since Danielus had tried the hospitals and police, I thought that I should give them a ring in case something had happened in the interim. I used my phone to connect to the internet and searched for the contact numbers of the hospitals in and around the town. The first place I tried was the newly opened St Andrews Community Hospital.

"Hello, NHS St Andrews Community Hospital, Sharon speaking."

"Hi, Sharon. I was wondering if you've had a young woman with memory loss or a serious head injury admitted in the last few days."

"What's her name?"

"It's Alicja but you might not have her name as she'll have forgotten it or been unable to tell you it."

She giggled. "Of course, sorry. I'll check for you."

I could hear the keys of a computer keyboard being tapped as she queried a database.

"No, sorry, we've not had anyone with that name or any injuries like that."

"Thanks for you help."

"You're welcome. Goodbye."

"Bye."

The calls to Ninewells Hospital in Dundee, Victoria Hospital in Kirkcaldy and Queen Margaret's in Dunfermline produced similar results. So I could rule out a head trauma as the reason for Alicja's mysterious disappearance unless she had gone far beyond the boundaries of Fife.

Calls to the local police stations were equally unproductive, which at least meant she hadn't been arrested.

Next on my list was the Polish consulate in Edinburgh. Once again I found the number on the web, then touched the link to dial.

"Consulate General of The Republic of Poland, Rahel speaking, how may I help you?" The young woman spoke English very precisely but with a distinctly Polish accent.

I had already decided to tell a shortened version of the story. "Hello, I'm wondering if you can help. I am looking for a friend of mine, Alicja Symanski. She's a Polish citizen and she's not been in contact with any of her friends or family for nearly a week. I was wondering if she had been in touch with the consulate?"

"One moment, please," the woman replied.

A couple of minutes of hold muzak corrupted my ears before a man's voice was heard on the line. "Fryderyk Kucharski, vice-consul. How may I help you?" His accent was slight, there was even a touch of Scots burr in it, as if he had lived here for a few years.

"My name is Craig Campbell. As I was explaining to your colleague, I am looking for a Polish friend of mine who has gone missing. Her name is Alicja Symanski. I was wondering if she has she been in touch with you at all?"

There was a pause as if he was looking for information. "No, I'm afraid not Mr Campbell, no one of that name has been in touch with us. Has she been missing for a long time?"

"She was last seen last Saturday night at a party."

"That is not so good. If you give me your number, I will contact you if I or any of my colleagues hear anything from her."

I gave him my mobile number and thanked him for his assistance.

*

I strolled along the short distance to the Drouthy Neebors at twenty past twelve: I found a table close to the door after ordering an orange juice. The pub was traditional in style and felt very welcoming. The smell of lunch being prepared pervaded the air and the excited buzz of people anticipating the weekend filled every corner.

Hero arrived five minutes after I did.

"Gerard's on his way, can I get you another drink?" he offered.

I declined and waited while he ordered a glass of sparkling water for himself. He had barely sat down when an intensely serious man approached the table. He was clutching a briefcase that looked like an antique: the tanned leather was cracked like the bark of an ancient tree. He held it like a warrior's shield in front of him, protecting him from some imagined threat.

"Gerard, this is Craig Campbell, the detective I texted you about."

"Hello. A pleasure to meet you, Mr Campbell." He greeted me with courtly formality.

"The usual?" Hero asked.

"Yes please." The answer was enough to establish his roots as being in the Home Counties of England.

I scrutinised him as he took off his Barbour wax jacket and settled into the chair. He was a couple of stone overweight and looked at least ten years older than a man who had just turned twenty-one. His hair was somewhere between brown and black in colour, greasy and plastered tightly to his head, like a swimming cap for hell's water polo team. His eyes were also a deep brown, wide like he had been startled by something. They were enclosed behind a pair of wire-framed spectacles that did nothing to help to dispel the image that he projected of a thirty-year-old banker. There was the slightest hint of a sheen of sweat on his forehead, whether it was from nerves or exertion I couldn't tell.

He was dressed in a pink formal shirt, open at the neck, a navy blue woollen jumper over the shirt, a pair of dark corduroy trousers and a pair of plain black boots. The logo of some club or maybe a school adorned the left breast of the pullover.

When Hero had returned with Gerard's pint of lager, I asked one of my regular questions. "Is it OK

54

if I record our conversation?"

"That's fine." He sounded both tense and timid.

I set the recorder in its customary position between my interviewee and myself.

"Hero said you might be able to help me with some information about one of your guests on Saturday night. She's a Polish girl, Alicja is her name."

I reached into my backpack and pulled out the picture of Alicja and Stefania.

"Alicja's the girl on the left."

He took the photo from me and stared at it, biting his lip as he considered the girls.

"Yes, I think I recognise them both. I've seen this one," he tapped Stefania's face, "somewhere with one of my lecturers, Doctor Barclay. I thought she was a student. The girl you're looking for was at the party, I think. It's hard to be sure, there were so many people. I didn't know half of them. It wasn't my idea to have a party but some of my classmates insisted and Hero organised it for me." He looked as if the celebration of his birthday had been akin to torture at the hands of the Inquisition. I could understand Hero's reaction to my question earlier about Gerard and the partygoers.

"Gerard's a bit on the shy side, we're trying to bring him out of his shell." Hero intimated, grinning. His ribbing seemed good natured but Gerard wasn't convinced.

There was a brief exchange of looks between

them before Gerard continued. "I remember now, the girl on the left was talking to one of the guys I was at school with. He's at the university as well. His name is Rupert Haines."

"Were they together as a couple?"

"Em... I don't know." The subtleties of social interaction were probably not one of Gerard's strengths.

"Would I be able to talk to him?"

"You could come with me today if you want. I meet him for a game of putting at the Himalayas on a Friday afternoon."

The Himalayas is the unofficial name for The Ladies' Putting Club of St Andrews. A formidable challenge of putting skill, it sits adjacent to the second tee of the Old Course. I had spent many a happy hour on that very green, trying to defeat my dad when I was a kid .

"OK, I can do that, if your friend doesn't mind." I replied.

"No, I think that should be fine. Do you play?"

"I think I can manage a round of putting," I said in a more condescending tone than I probably should have used.

"Rupert likes to have a wager. He usually wins." It was said with little relish, his admiration for his friend's victories was hardly a glowing tribute to his skills.

"I'll bear that in mind."

His thoughts then turned to food and he ordered

a cheeseburger with a large portion of chips on the side, Hero settled for a panini. I decided to pass as I had eaten in the café. Gerard set about demolishing his lunch quickly while Hero and I chatted about life as a student in St Andrews.

He told me that Gerard was the original occupant of the flat and that he had joined him when a previous flat mate left in January. I asked Hero about his exams and how his course was progressing. He seemed to enjoy university life and his studies were going well.

Gerard seemed oblivious to us as he attacked the burger with all the gusto of a hyena devouring the corpse of a zebra. They seemed an unlikely pair of flatmates but it obviously suited them both.

Around a quarter to two, Gerard had completed his meal and was ready to go to the putting green.

I thanked Hero for his help as we parted outside the pub. I walked with Gerard, exchanging small talk until we reached the green. The sun was trying hard to find a break in the clouds and the rain showers were now less frequent.

*

We arrived at the green about five minutes early for Gerard's appointment. He paid for three adults and we were handed our putters and balls. I left my rucksack and he gave his briefcase to the attendant in the small clubhouse.

My sense of nostalgia was heightened by being

back at the green. I hadn't played here for many years, it provoked joyful memories but even the happiest memories can be tainted by pain when they are of someone you miss.

"We'll wait a couple of minutes for Rupert," Gerard said.

I nodded and then turned my attention to the other players already out on the green.

I watched a couple in their seventies begin their round. They both seemed to be accomplished players and they acknowledged each other's best shots. They laughed and enjoyed the moment, their love expressed in little touches. It was a heartening sight, a romance so obvious in a couple their age.

The exposed area of the putting green was subject to the full force of the North Sea winds that were an almost constant in St Andrews. Gerard shivered as we waited.

Within a few minutes a towering, blonde-haired young man came down the steps to the starting area.

"Ah, here he is." Gerard seemed relieved that there was someone to break the uneasy silence that had descended between us.

"Chubs, how the hell are you, old chap?" Rupert's voice rolled like thunder, the precise pronunciation of an English public school education reverberating across the green with all the subtlety of a tidal wave.

"I'm good, thanks Rupert."

He turned his attention to me. "Who is this then?"

"My name's Craig Campbell, I'm a private detective." I offered a hand but it was ignored.

He laughed, a loud braying sound accompanied by a snort. "Really. What, have one of those fillies you tupped got one in the oven, Chubs? Or maybe he has some tasty pics to blackmail you with?"

Gerard's face blushed a fuchsia pink, his head tilted forward and he murmured an incoherent negative into his chest.

"Only kidding, Chubs. We think that Chubs bats for the other team, anyway. Isn't that right, Chubs?" He aimed a jovial punch at Gerard's arm while his victim's face turned from pink to ruby red.

I interrupted the bullying. "I'm here to ask some questions about a girl who went missing from a party you attended on Saturday night. Gerard thought that I might be able to join you in your game while we talked."

"Good show, as long as you've got some cash you are very welcome. Tenner in, winner takes all."

"That's fine by me."

"Shall we start?" He walked to the first hole marker, striding with the confidence that was bred in to his class, the air of a being who believes in his superiority over other lesser mortals regardless of evidence to the contrary. Gerard tagged on behind him, unable to resist the pull of his tormentor. I wondered how long the symbiotic relationship had existed between the two: Gerard's need for companionship was balanced by Rupert's need for a figure to browbeat, Gerard a moth to Rupert's torturing flame.

As Rupert lined up his first shot, I examined him. He was extremely tall, around six feet five inches I reckoned. The putter looked tiny in his great mitt of a hand. He wore a flat cap on his head and his hair, tinged with red, spilled in unruly locks from below it. His cheeks had the high colour flush of a small child who had come in from the cold to a warm room. A pair of cool blue eyes lay below the streaks of blonde hair that made up his eyebrows.

He was attired in clothes that his grandfather would have felt comfortable in, a tweed jacket over a pastel blue shirt with a lemon tie and waistcoat: his legs were encased in a heavy, brown moleskin and he had a pair of oxblood brogues on his feet. It was common in St Andrews to see any number of the student body dressed as if they had stepped out of a time machine from the nineteen thirties: like the fashions of the past eighty years had come and gone, leaving them singularly unimpressed.

He began the game and his first putt came to rest some eight feet from the hole. Gerard then stepped forward to take his shot.

"So you mentioned something about a girl from the party?" Rupert asked.

"Yes, her name is Alicja Symanski. She's Polish and works at the Rose Farm. Gerard and Hero thought you had spent some time with her on Saturday." I handed him Alicja's photograph and pointed her out before I took my first putt.

As we walked to take our second shots he said, "There were a lot of ladies keen to get their hands on some of the old Haines magic on Saturday night." My stomach pitched in nausea.

"Can you look at the picture, please?" I could feel my voice stressing as I tried to keep it under control.

We finished the hole with no advantage to anyone. He looked at the picture and pretended to consider it but the fact that he had indeed spoken to Alicja was written plainly across his face.

"Yes, I recall, we did have a chat."

"Can you remember anything about her?"

"I thought she was one of Michaels' eewops?"

"Eewops?"

"You know Eastern European Wop, as opposed to an Italian one. It's my pet name for them, like the cute little Ewok creatures in Star Wars. Frightfully clever, I thought." He smiled like a five-year-old presenting his latest finger painting to his doting mother.

I ignored the comment. "Michael?"

"Michaels. Robbie Michaels, I think his name is. He runs a lap dancing club in Dundee. Some of his girls do some extra curricular work, if you catch my drift."

"You mean he's a pimp."

"I wouldn't say that exactly. The girls accompany those who, unlike myself, struggle with the opposite sex." His face again returned to its default expression, a smug grin.

"Escorts then?"

"Yes, that's the word."

I won the second hole with two putts to my opponents' three. As a result Rupert's demeanour slipped from jovial affability to a distinctly unfriendly peevishness.

As we played round the course, I continued to probe for something that might help me with what had happened to Alicja.

"So you hadn't met Alicja before that night, at another party maybe?"

"No, not that I remember anyway. I go to so many parties and balls. I meet loads of fine young ladies."

"Was there any indication from her that she was involved with Michaels?"

"No. I just assumed as she was from behind the old iron curtain. I thought maybe someone had hired her and abandoned her, ran out of cash kind of thing."

"What's the name of this club?"

"The Starlight Club, it's in the old Tay Hotel building, not far from the railway station," he replied confidently, as if he had intimate knowledge of the place.

"I think I know where that is. How do you get in touch with these escorts then?"

"There's a number to call, a guy I know has used the service. Ugly sod he is, face like Jabba the Hutt's arse. The only way a decent bit of tottie would be seen on his arm is if he paid her." The donkey laugh once again disrupted the peace of the tranquil scene.

"Can you get it to me, please? It might be important."

"Yes, will do."

We continued the game, it was tightly contested and the result came down to the final hole. Gerard had won two holes, while Rupert and I were tied on three holes apiece. Rupert putted up to within four feet, Gerard then followed but was a bit further away. I rolled mine up to roughly equidistant to Rupert's but on the other side of the hole. Gerard missed his second, I was next to play. There was a left to right break on the putt that took my shot to the right of the hole, where it caught the lip and rolled around the cup once before dropping to the bottom. Rupert's putt broke the other way but was slightly down hill, which made it more difficult. His swing was slightly too long and although he also caught the lip, the ball spun away.

I had won the match, much to the disgust of at least one of my playing partners. As Rupert walked away, Gerard cracked a huge smile at his departing back. When we reached the clubhouse again, Rupert pulled his wallet from the inside pocket of his jacket and thrust a ten pound note towards me with as little grace as he could muster. Gerard also offered me my winnings, I took ten pounds from my own wallet, folded it with the other two and put it into the RNLI collecting tin that was sitting on the clubhouse counter. This seemed to annoy Rupert even more, which delighted me as much as it irritated him.

We began the walk back to town with Haines trailing behind, sulking, while I asked Gerard about his studies. We walked past the Royal & Ancient Clubhouse. It was first built in 1853 and has been extended six times over the years. It is now the one of the most recognisable buildings in sport and would be the backdrop for the climax of the Open Championship that July. The stands were already being constructed to cope with the influx of fans from around the globe.

When we reached the golf museum on the opposite side of Golf Place from the clubhouse, I said goodbye to the two students, reminding Rupert about the phone number. He grunted a reply that I took to be an affirmative response.

"Thanks for your help, Gerard."

"Thanks for the game, I really enjoyed it." I hoped his smile wouldn't be wiped from his face by his so-called friend when I left him.

I was back at the bike within ten minutes. Within an hour I was opening my mother's door.

*

As Mum was out, I brewed up the Chiapas coffee I had purchased the previous day. I typed up my notes on the computer but it had been a less than productive day. The connection to the strip club seemed tenuous but at least it was possible that it was worthy of further investigation. There had been so little to go on thus far that I wondered if I would ever be able to get to the bottom of Alicja's disappearance.

When I had finished with the notes, I caught up on some e-mail. There was nothing else I could do, so I decided to have another cup of coffee and switched on the television.

I settled on the BBC news channel, which was running an almost constant commentary on the coming election. A parade of chinless wonders representing their own party's views, fully analysed by another collection of characterless people with their own agenda to promote. It bored me, politics had become a vehicle to advance the candidates' careers: what colour of tie or which blouse you wore was more important than policies that benefitted all the country. The days of conviction politicians who served the needs of their constituents had disappeared with the arrival of 24-hour television news channels.

As I was reaching for the remote to change the channel, a breaking news banner began to scroll across the screen.

Body found on a beach in Fife.

A chill ran through me as the possibilities and implications became apparent. There were five minutes more of repetitive boring political analysis before the newsreader changed the topic and began to add some details to the headline.

"A report is coming in of a woman's body having

been found on the beach at Tentsmuir Forest, near Leuchars in Fife. We cross to our reporter, Janice Lorimer, who is at the scene."

The picture switched to a woman in her early thirties, dressed in a stone-coloured raincoat. She was standing in the drizzle, crime scene tape blocking the road behind her, the sand of the expanse of beach visible beyond the tape. Police officers and scene of crime technicians in white overalls were already at work in and around a protective tent, keeping the scene as dry and undisturbed as they could. Flood-lights had been erected to allow the officers, patholo-gists and forensic team to carry on their work even as the light faded.

My mother walked in behind me as the reporter relayed the information, "Hello, son."

"Quiet, Mum. I need to hear this."

She paused behind the sofa and listened with me.

"Thanks, Jeremy. Yes, we have very few particu-lars but we believe the naked body of a young woman was discovered by a man walking his dog on the beach at about midday today."

"Have the police any idea where this body may have come from?" the man in the studio asked.

"Not at the moment but in a brief conversa-tion with a local forest ranger, he told me that the sea and estuaries around this area are notorious for their unpredictable and ever changing currents. There are many shifting sandbars that affect the currents which, he believed, meant a body could have come from anywhere within a thirty-mile stretch of coastline. The other possibility, of course, is that the woman was thrown from a passing boat or ship, so this could be a very difficult investigation for the police."

"What about the man who found her? Has he been able to supply any details?"

"Well, Jeremy, the gentleman concerned was so shocked that he was rushed to Ninewells Hospital in Dundee with a suspected heart attack. I believe they will keep him in overnight for observation."

"Thanks, Janice. We will bring you more on this story when we get it. Now for the sport."

I switched off the TV.

"Is that the girl you're looking for?"

"I honestly don't know, Mum. I hope not."

"You told me this wasn't going to be dangerous," she admonished.

"We don't know this has anything to do with my case, it might be an accident or something that has nothing to do with Alicja."

"An accident! She took her clothes off before having an accident." She exclaimed her disbelief.

I held my hands up to placate her. "Well, she might have been skinny dipping and got caught in a current or maybe it's a suicide, we just don't know."

"Oh God, what am I going to do with you?"

"Let me make dinner and you can tell me about

your day."

I busied myself in the kitchen preparing some breast of chicken, potatoes and broccoli with a white wine sauce. My mother ran through the gossip she had heard from her visit to the local tearoom, while I indicated an occasional agreement or exclamation of shock, where I thought it was appropriate. In truth, my mind was occupied by the dead woman and considering the possibility that it meant the end of my case.

Over dinner I told Mum of my visit to the putting green.

She smiled, "You and your Dad would play there practically every day when we were at the caravan."

"I remember it well. It was a strange feeling being back."

"You were just beginning to be able to beat your Dad before he died." Her sad smile reflected my own feelings.

"Do you still miss him as much as you used to?"

"Aye, son. That won't change."

"Did you ever think of maybe finding someone else? You were still young when he died."

She shook her head. "No. There was no man that could give me what I had with your father and it would have been unfair to let anyone try. I was lucky, I met and married my soulmate. We had a great life together, even if it was too short."

I added my own thoughts. "I miss him but most of

all I wonder what else we would have shared. There's so much of my life he missed, things we would have talked about and laughed about."

"I know, son. There's many in the world who should have gone before your father but there's no justice. It's why I lost faith in any God, if a good man like your father could suffer and die the way he did while the rogues are still here, how can there be a God who is kind and loving?"

We both retreated into our own memories as we finished the meal.

Dinner completed and dishes washed, I retreated to the spare room and tried to call Danielus but his phone was off or he was out of range. I decided to try calling him again the following morning and to take him to the police to see if his and my own worst fears would be realised.

I phoned Carol again, pleased to hear her voice. I talked about my day, including the gruesome discovery on the beach. I also talked about the memories of my Dad that my round of putting had inspired. It was probably the most I had said about him to her since we had been together. The conversation lasted an hour and I felt that it had a cathartic effect on me. Sharing a little of my life before we met helped to bring us that bit closer.

The case was still gnawing away at me and the concern that the body was Alicja was at the forefront of my thoughts.

I spent the rest of the night watching a movie

on the laptop, leaving my mother to choose her own viewing for the evening. I fell asleep with the laptop still running and woke up in the middle of the night with it perched on my chest. I gained little rest from a night of morbid theories and dreadful imaginings.

SATURDAY 17TH APRIL, 2010

I was up and dressed before seven thirty on the Saturday morning, my body aching from a lack of sleep: I had struggled to find a comfortable position in bed that would have allowed me to relax. I prepared a simple breakfast, a slice of toast and a cup of coffee, before switching on the television again.

There were no new details, other than a brief statement from the police saying that no one had been able to identify the body and that the gentleman who had discovered the woman was due to be released from hospital: the fear of a heart attack had proved to be unfounded.

By eight o'clock I thought I should give Danielus a call. The phone rang six times before he answered.

"Hi Danielus, it's Craig."

"Good morning." He sounded sleepy and slightly unsettled, as if he too had woken from a disturbing dream.

"Have you seen or heard the news since yester-day evening?" I asked.

"No. Has something happened?"

"A woman's body has been found on a beach not far from St Andrews."

"Oh." There was a long, deep silence at the other end of the line, his voice stilled by the unwanted but dreaded information.

"Are you still there?"

"Yes, sorry. Do you think it is Alicja?" The emotion he was feeling gave his voice a vibrato quality as he strained to keep himself from breaking down.

"I hope not but I think we have to consider the possibility. We should go to the police and see if they will allow us to see the woman's body. They haven't identified who it is yet, you might be able to help."

"OK, yes you're right. We need to try and help." He could not have sounded any more unwilling.

"I'll come and get you, we can go to the police together."

"Yes. Thank you, that would be a help." He sounded relieved that he wouldn't have to face the ordeal on his own.

"I'll pick you up in about an hour."

"I will be ready. Goodbye."

As I hung up, Mum walked into the living room.

"Are you going out?"

"Yes, I'm taking Danielus, the man who hired

72

me, to the police. He might be able to identify the body of the woman washed up on the beach."

"Craig, I'm worried about you." She rubbed her arms in front of her body, a gesture I remembered well from the time of my father's illness. It was her anxious stance, the pose she struck when things were out of her control.

I reassured her. "Mum, if it is Alicja, my involvement will be over, the police will handle it."

"I suppose you're right but please be careful."

"I will, I promise." I kissed her gently on the cheek, she managed a weak smile in return.

Before I left, I called Fife Constabulary who advised me that the body would have been transferred to the mortuary in Dundee. They arranged for two officers to meet Danielus and me at the mortuary at eleven thirty, the post-mortem was to be carried out at two that afternoon.

As I was about to climb on the bike my phone rang again. Carol's name and photograph appeared on the display.

"Hi, darling. How are you today?"

"I'm good. Missing you but apart from that good. What are you up to today?"

"I'm going to take Danielus to Dundee Mortuary to see if the girl they found is Alicja."

"That'll be tough. I'll keep my fingers crossed that it isn't her. I'll speak to you later. Love you."

"Love you, too. Bye."

*

73

The ride to the farm was problem free and I arrived at quarter past nine. Danielus was waiting for me at the end of the path leading to his temporary home. His face was creased in concern but he seemed to be bracing himself for what might lie ahead.

"Hello Craig, I am ready to go."

"We have to meet a Detective Constable Gray and one of his colleagues at the mortuary at eleven thirty. Are you sure you're OK to do this?"

"I have never seen a dead body before. I am a little nervous and I pray that it is not my friend." He crossed himself, his religion an old anchor to cling to.

"Me too. Let's head."

I gave him the spare helmet from my luggage case, he climbed on to the pillion and gripped my jacket fiercely. Normally, I would have suggested we use his car but having seen it, I wasn't convinced it was the safest thing on the road or that it would manage the journey to Dundee without a catastrophic mechanical collapse.

As we passed through St Andrews, a haar had descended on the town like something from a Stephen King novel. It was a typical sudden change in the weather around a town that seemed to have its own microclimate. The temperature had dropped about 10 degrees between leaving the farm and passing through the centre of town. The grey buildings disappeared like the cottages of Brigadoon, camouflaged by the thickening mist. However, by the time we had reached Leuchars, the air was clearing and we were once again out into the spring light, the air was feeling warmer again.

As we crossed the bridge, the fog had also found its way to the Tay estuary, a white ribbon of cotton wool resting gently on the silver river. It was like flying above the clouds as we rode out of Fife towards the City of Discovery.

Dundee was bathed in a watery sunshine as we made our way down off the bridge. A glance at my watch told me that it was only quarter to eleven. I steered the bike up to Bell Street and found a parking space. It was too early to go straight to our appointment, so we ambled back towards the main shopping area of the city.

As we walked, two teenage boys swaggered towards us. They were both dressed in tracksuits, one a festive green the other a fire engine red. It was like Santa had decided to hire neds instead of elves for his workshop. I smiled at the thought as we continued our walk.

I noticed a cafe in the McManus Museum, which was only a short distance from the mortuary in West Bell Street.

"Fancy a coffee?" I wanted to take Danielus' mind off of the task at hand.

Danielus was obviously distracted but the question eventually registered and he answered with a simple nod.

We went into the beautiful Victorian building

that had recently been refurbished. It served as both an art gallery and the repository for the social history of Dundee and its people. The restaurant area is on the right as you enter through the main door.

We settled in to our seats and a cheery plump woman in her late forties took our order. Danielus chose a peppermint tea, while I opted for an Americano coffee. As we waited, I began a gentle interrogation of Danielus.

"What's life like on the farm, then?"

He considered his answer before he replied. "It is hard work. There are good people, I have made many friends, including Alicja, but there are also people who are not so nice."

"You mean Bennett?"

"Yes. He is a very rude man and he treats us very badly."

"Have you told Colin Rose about it?"

"Mr Rose sees only his friend, he cannot see the real person. There is no point complaining or I would lose my job."

"Has someone else lost their job for complaining?"

"We have had many people leave since Mr Bennett was made our boss." He answered cryptically.

I paused the conversation as the waitress arrived with our order.

When she had gone I continued, "Are many of those who leave women?"

"Nearly all of them are women. The only man to have started since Mr Bennett was put in charge is George. I think sometimes, that the only reason he picked George was so he could abuse him. He calls him terrible names."

"What kind of names?"

"He calls George kaffir and nigger, awful things like that." He shook his head with disgust, a distaste I could relate to.

"What about you? I've already seen him use some derogatory terms about you."

"What you heard was not so bad. He calls me other things that are about me being gay, they are much worse than the other day. Not everyone in Scotland is more tolerant."

"No, I'm afraid not. Has he ever been violent towards you or anyone else?" I was trying to get a fix on Bennett, something tangible that I could move forward with.

"No, not to me and I haven't heard of it if he has. I think he is like many people who bully, they are truly cowards at heart."

"Do you think that he has made sexual advances towards the women? Maybe that is the main reason they left the farm."

"I don't know for sure but he certainly makes disgusting remarks to the women, about their breasts and other sex comments."

Bennett was moving into my sights rapidly.

"Tell me more about Alicja, what kind of person is she?"

"She is someone who likes to laugh. She is a good listener and cares for her friends. She is a wonderful singer, a clear voice that I love to listen to. I think that she brightens a room when she is in it. She loves her family, they are the most important thing to her. She is very worried about her father, he suffers from the shaking disease, I cannot remember the name."

"Parkinson's?" I suggested.

"Yes, I think that is it. She works hard to make the money to support her Papa, her brother is in Germany to also make money to help him."

"Has anyone contacted her brother?"

"I haven't but maybe her Mama would have told him."

I felt that there was certainly plenty to investigate further and that Danielus was already concerned enough about what we were about to do without me quizzing him about every detail. I decided to change the subject.

"Where in Lithuania are you from?"

"I was born in Rasos, close to Vilnius, but I lived in the capital most of my life."

"Do you have a big family?"

"No, there was only Daina and me, although I have many cousins."

"What drove you to come to Scotland?"

"My father is very strict in his religion. He

believes me to be evil because I am gay. I have tried to explain that I was born this way, this is the way God made me, but he does not listen. We had many arguments and finally he told me to leave his house. I think he needed to be angry with someone as there was no one to blame for Daina's death. Not that he blames me but my sexuality gives him a target. My mother tried to get him to change his mind but he is a very stubborn man. My mother hoped our priest would change his mind but he agreed with my father.

I found a flat in Vilnius while I was a student but I was hassled there by some people who are very scared of gay people. They are like Nazis, they hate everything that is different. I thought that Britain would be better and there was an agency, close to where I lived, who helped people to find work in Scotland. I knew this is a beautiful country and decided I would like to work here."

"What did you do at home?"

"I am a graphics artist, for advertising mostly."

"It's very different work you're doing now."

"It is but maybe when the economy is better I will get a better job. Apart from Mr Bennett, I have enjoyed my time here."

I checked my watch and realised it was eleven twenty. I paid the bill and we strolled the short distance back to the mortuary. Danielus was once again quiet during the walk and I left him to his own thoughts.

The Dundee mortuary is situated close to the Tayside Police HQ. It looks more like a compact country cottage than an important public building. The police HQ towers above it like a protective big brother. It is constructed of blonde sandstone and a short flight of steps takes you up to the door that occupies the centre of the structure, a disabled ramp on the opposite also leads up to the door. It is managed by Dundee University and supplies services for the whole of Tayside and a large part of Fife.

I pressed the intercom button and explained who we were and why we were there. A short time later the door was opened by a middle-aged man, wearing a blue suit, white shirt and striped tie.

"Come in. I'm Detective Sergeant Tulloch, I'm one of the investigating officers."

We followed him into a small hall with a number of doors leading off it. We shook the policeman's hand as we introduced ourselves before he led us into a room marked Family Waiting Area. There was another man inside the room and he introduced himself to us.

"Hi, I'm Detective Constable Gray." He was very small for a policeman, around 5 feet 8 inches tall. I reckoned that he was in his early thirties. His near black curly hair and ebony eyes contrasted with his pale skin: dressed in a black suit, white shirt and black tie, he was like a character from a Chaplin film that had stepped from the screen into real life. His ears were prominent and stuck out from beneath the curls. His lips were a thin, pink line under a sharp nose.

"Hi, I'm Craig Campbell and this is Danielus Petrauskas."

"I'll check if the pathologist is ready for us," DS Tulloch said before he walked out the door again.

"You think you might be able to help us with the identification of the body that was found on the beach?" DC Gray asked Danielus.

"Maybe. I am hoping that it is not my friend but I have to find out. Mr Campbell is helping me to look for her."

"Yes, he told my colleague on the phone. We will wait until the Sergeant comes back and then we'll take you through. The woman is in another room, you will view her through a window. We will simply ask you if you can identify her."

He offered us both a cup of tea but we declined. I looked around the room. It felt more homely than bureaucratic, with a royal blue carpet, two wallpapers separated by a dado rail and tasteful art on the walls. It was a room no one wanted to be in and it wouldn't make you feel any better but at least there was a humanity to it that gave it a reassuring warmth.

Tulloch was back within five minutes.

"We can go through now. If you would follow me, please."

We did as instructed and he escorted us through to a room with two chairs. There was a plain blue curtain in front of a window. DC Gray indicated the seats and invited us to sit down.

The senior detective then took control. "The woman we found was in the water for four days. I'm afraid that being in the water for that amount of time has taken a heavy toll on her, as you can imagine. When I open the curtain you will see her on the other side of the glass. Her face will be visible but the rest of her body is covered."

Danielus was, by now, shaking quite visibly. I felt a similar anxiety myself although not to the same degree.

The policeman walked to the curtain and slowly pulled a cord to open it.

"Take your time and look carefully."

A spotlight was focused on the face of the woman. A female pathologist stood behind the body, partially hidden by the way the horrific cameo was lit.

I studied the face as closely as I could, dispelling my own fear in an attempt to be professional.

The light cast a harsh glare on the features of the woman. It was difficult to estimate her age. She had taken on a bloated appearance from the time she had spent in the sea. Her features were distended, her skin a bluish white and almost transparent. The veins were prominent across the area of skin we could see, giving it the look of Italian marble. It was difficult to believe that she wasn't some renaissance statue the sea had returned from some ancient wreck. Her long black hair had begun to loosen from the skin that was beginning to separate from her flesh. The majority of her hair hung limply from her head and lay on the trolley, dull and lifeless, like seaweed stranded on the rocks.

I turned to look at Danielus, who was now trembling. "No, it is not her. The hair is too long and it is the wrong colour." He started to cry, the fear mingling with relief to burst the dam of his emotions.

"Are you sure Mr Petrauskas? It is very important. "

Danielus nodded his head, definite in his response.

Gray reached over to hide the terrible visage by closing the curtain, ending the macabre show.

DS Tulloch opened the door again and we stepped out into the waiting area. "OK, thank you. I realise that it must be very difficult for you and I hope you find your friend safe and well soon." There was disappointment for him as the investigation would be infinitely more difficult if they couldn't identify the poor woman.

We sat for about ten minutes, no one saying anything as Danielus wrestled with his feelings. When he had calmed a little the detective led us out to the outside door, thanked us again and we parted.

Even as we walked, Danielus was still struggling to compose himself after the painful experience. He spoke for a short time in Lithuanian, as if reciting a prayer of some sort.

"Are you OK, Danielus?"

"I am sorry, I was thinking of that girl's family. How terrible it is, the thing that happened to her. I feel guilty for being relieved that it is not Alicja. There is a still someone who will be looking for that woman, they will not get the relief that I feel. Am I a dreadful person, Craig?"

"No, Danielus you are just human. We are all relieved when bad things happen to other people, even when we feel sympathy for them. It's only natural."

As we walked back to the bike he began to compose himself again. He didn't say any more, so I left him alone with his thoughts.

My own feelings were equally conflicting. Somewhere a mother would discover the death of her daughter, a brother the loss of his sister or maybe even a child the death of their mother. However, no matter how much I sympathised, there was nothing I could for them or the poor woman in the mortuary. The only person I had to concern myself with was Alicja.

*

We were back at the farm within the hour. As Danielus returned the helmet to the luggage box, he looked drained of energy by the trauma of our trip.

"Can we see if Stefania is about? I'd like to ask her some questions."

"I will check."

He walked the short distance to the girls' caravan but before he could knock, the door swung open. Stefania was standing at the top of the steps. She was still dressed in her nightwear, a pair of pink pyjamas covered by a black silk dressing gown. Her hair was now black with tints of shocking pink: it looked like a bramble bush, sharp thorns of gelled strands sticking out in every direction. There was no sign of the child's doll face now, she was all spiky belligerence, but it was all for show. Her face was devoid of make-up and the only way I knew for sure it was her was the line of piercings on her ear that I recognised from the photograph.

"Well?" she asked urgently.

"It was not her." Danielus said with a sigh of relief.

There were a couple of sentences of Polish from Stefania as she made the sign of the cross over her chest three times, the facade crumbled and the vulnerable, scared woman appeared.

"Stefania, this is Craig Campbell, he is the man who is looking for Alicja. He would like to talk to you about her. Craig, this is Stefania Nowakowski."

"Hi." I said.

"Hello, please come in." She walked away from the door to allow us access to the caravan.

The curtains were still drawn and the interior was dark. Danielus noticed the gloom and reached to switch on the light.

Stefania sat on the couch at the end of the living space, her face even paler in the artificial light. Danielus and I took station on the chairs in the dining area.

She was huddled in an upright foetal position, legs close to her chest, her arms wrapped round her legs. She was hauntingly slender, her bones thrust hard against her ivory skin as if they were trying to escape from their delicate casing.

"Are you OK, Stefania?"

"Yes. I worry about Alicja." Her accent was very pronounced. There was a hesitancy, as if she wasn't confident speaking English.

"Can I ask you about Neil Bennett?" I asked gently. She looked so fragile that the wrong tone of voice might have shattered her completely, like a porcelain doll.

"He is horrible man. What about him?" Even the mention of his name had sparked a fierce response.

"You sort of answered my question. How does he behave towards you?"

"He is disgusting pig. He make rude suggestions and touches us on bottom. He is pervert." She spat the words as if removing a bad taste from her mouth, the fragility cast aside for a second as she reacted to a vile stimulus.

"What kind of rude suggestions?" I felt like I needed to tread carefully, I didn't want her too angry as it could be difficult to get information from her if she wasn't in control of her emotions.

"He picks up carrot and holds it between legs. He say 'you like to lick my tasty carrot' and other things like that."

"Has he ever been violent towards anyone?"

"No, just pervert, that is bad enough."

"There have been a lot of women that have moved away from the farm recently." I stated.

"Yes. They just say one day they have new job and disappear. They are sick of the pig." The last word was full of venom.

"Did Alicja ever mention leaving?"

"We talked about it many times but we need money. We worry that we won't find new job."

"OK. Tell me about Saturday, before Alicja went missing."

"We finished work at four. We had some dinner and we get dressed for party. Alicja had bought a new dress. We were ready about seven, I think. We had taxi booked to take us to town. Alicja was nervous and excited about something, she will not say why. I thought she had new boyfriend but she would not tell me. I was angry at her, she acted foolish. We had argument in car."

Her emotional response flipped again. Small beads of tears formed at the corner of her eyes.

"What was the argument about?"

"It was nothing important." She shook her head

but the lie was drawn across her face.

"It must have been something important if it makes you feel like this." I coaxed her.

"No, I cannot say, it is a private thing."

"It might be important, Stefania. It might help me to find Alicja, you need to help me."

"It is private." She shouted back to me before burying her face in her hands.

Danielus went to comfort her. "Stefania, Mr Campbell is trying to help. We must find Alicja. If you know something you must tell him. There is no point in secrets if it stops us from getting Alicja back."

"I know, I know. It is not easy for me. She is like sister for many years."

"What happened in the taxi, Stefania?" I demanded forcefully.

"We had stupid argument about my boyfriend."

"Your boyfriend. Who would that be?"

"It is one of the men who work at university in town."

"Would that be Doctor Barclay by any chance?" I queried.

She looked shocked. "How did you know that?"

"Someone I spoke to said that he had seen you with him around the town."

"I thought we were, what is word, descreet?"

"Discreet, yes."

"Yes. We tell no one."

"Why? Is Doctor Barclay married?"

Once again her mouth opened wide to express her surprise. "How do you know this?"

"It wasn't difficult to guess, Stefania. So why were you arguing with Alicja?"

"I don't know. She was acting strange, silly, like little girl on birthday. I was annoyed, told her to stop it. She was angry with me then and told me that I was the one being silly. She said that Roger would not love me, would not be with me. He was a bad man who only wanted me for sex. I told her that she was wrong, she did not know him. He would leave his wife for me, he promised me." The realisation that Alicja was right seemed to enfold her suddenly. The sad truth of her relationship had been placed in a glaring spotlight by the words of her friend.

"What happened then?"

"She said she would test him. She would tell his wife that he was with me."

"Did you tell Doctor Barclay this?"

"Yes. I could not go to party, I was very upset. I phoned him on his cell phone. He was very angry at me for calling him when he was with his wife. He said he would call me later after he had spoken to Alicja. I got taxi back here. He called on Sunday, said he did not see Alicja and that it was over for us. He was still angry with me." She cried gently into Danielus' chest.

"How did that make you feel? Were you angry

with Alicja?"

"Yes, of course."

"Did you go back into town on Saturday night?"

"No. I stay here."

"Can anyone vouch for you? Was there anyone with you?"

"No. What do you suggest? That I would hurt Alicja? You are crazy man." She was very angry at my line of questioning.

"I'm just trying to establish the facts. What about your man friend? Are you worried that he has done something to harm Alicja?"

"I do not know, he said he didn't see her but he was very angry. Before, I had never heard him like that. He was always gentle." Her doubts about Barclay were easy to identify in her voice.

"OK, Stefania. I will find out what happened on Saturday."

"I hope she is OK. I miss her very much, I do not know what I do if she can't come back. It was stupid to argue over man who did not love me. But I could not hurt her, believe me."

"I'll do the best that I can to bring her back. Do you have the Doctor's phone number?"

"Yes." She disappeared towards the bedroom and came back with her mobile phone. I gave her my number and she sent me the contact details I needed.

"If there is anything else you remember from Saturday or before, call me."

"I will."

"I better go, goodbye Stefania."

"Goodbye."

"I will come see you later Stefania," Danielus said as we left.

Outside, the sun was bright and small birds sang the joyful tunes of spring. In stark contrast, Danielus' expression was dark, an eclipse of concern.

"Do you think this man has hurt Alicja?"

"I don't think we should jump to any conclusions but he certainly has a motive. It's the first concrete thing we've learned, so it might be a start."

"Yes, but that is a week now. It does not look good."

"Try to remain positive, there might be an innocent explanation." I lied as well as I could but there was no doubt that the chances of finding her unharmed were diminishing by the day.

As we stood in the shadow of the caravan, a broad-shouldered African man walked down the hill towards us. He was very dark skinned, about five feet eight inches tall. He was wrapped in the familiar high-visibility jacket over a pair of very dusty dungarees.

Danielus noticed him. "Ah George, my friend, this is Mr Campbell. He is trying to help me to find Alicja."

George offered a grime-covered hand, the size of a garden shovel. I shook it before he realised that it was so dirty.

"My apologies, Mr Campbell. I have just finished work." His voice had a rich deep timbre, like a rolling log trundling through a forest.

"That's OK, and please, call me Craig."

"Are you having any luck finding Alicja?" he asked with genuine concern.

"Unfortunately not. Although Stefania may have given me some help today. Do you know Alicja well?"

"A little. We work together. She is a very nice person."

"How long have you known her?"

"About two months. I think. She was here when I arrived from Ghana. I come to work to make life better for my wife and children in Ghana." There was a pride in his words.

"Can you think of anyone who might want to harm Alicja?"

"No, she is a good girl, no one would want to hurt her, I don't think. She is a very kind person."

"What about Bennett?"

He looked at me strangely, fighting to keep his emotions in check. "I don't want to speak about this man. He has no honour, no respect. In Ghana I would do something about him but I do not want trouble here." His anger seethed just below the surface.

"I understand. Is there anything you could tell me that might help? Something you may have noticed or someone strange around the farm?"

"I am afraid not. I work, I eat, I sleep."

"If there's anything that occurs to you, no matter how small or trivial please get in touch, Danielus has my number."

"OK." He seemed to be a man of few words, an intensely private person.

"Thanks."

"I must go and get cleaned up. Goodbye, Craig."

He was already heading to his own caravan by the time I returned the greeting.

"George is a very quiet man. He is shy, I think." Danielus said.

"It can't be easy for him or any of you, being so far from home."

"It's not too bad for me but George misses his children. He works here to support them but he wishes they were here or he was with them."

"I better get going, I need to think about how to approach Barclay."

"I am worried for my friend. I think I might never see her again."

"Keep your chin up, there's still hope." I wished I had more to offer than mere words.

I patted Danielus on the shoulder and walked to the bike. As I passed the main farmyard, I noticed an old, green Land Rover sitting outside the Rose's house. As I hadn't seen it before, I thought that it might belong to Colin Rose. It seemed like a good opportunity to talk to him, to learn some more about Alicja and maybe Bennett.

My knock on the front door was greeted by the clatter of galloping paws hurtling towards the source of the sound. Someone shouted at the pack to get out of their way.

The door was opened by a man in his late thirties. He was stocky, with a broad head and a barrel chest. He strained as he tried to hold back a particularly enthusiastic mongrel that had a hint of Labrador in its genes.

"Hi, I'm Craig Campbell, I'm the private detective that Danielus has hired to look for Alicja."

"Oh, yes. I'm Colin Rose. Come in. Away you go." He shouted at his canine companions, who trotted away reluctantly.

I followed him into the same room that I had interviewed his father in. There was a smell of roast chicken drifting through from the kitchen which made my mouth water.

"Do you want a tea or coffee?"

"No, thanks, I'm fine."

As he walked to the kitchen his father came in the other direction.

"Good afternoon, Craig. Do you have any news?"

"Well, Danielus and I were at the mortuary this morning to look at the body that was washed up at Tentsmuir."

"Yes?"

"It wasn't Alicja, although it would be difficult

to say who it is. Danielus was convinced, due to her hair, that she wasn't Alicja but her face was a gruesome mess."

"Poor soul but it's a relief that it wasn't Alicja."

Colin shouted from the kitchen. "Dad, do you want tea or coffee?"

"Tea, please son."

"So what have you learned, so far?"

"A little bit here or there but it's piecing it into some kind of complete picture that is proving difficult."

"Do you think that someone has hurt her?"

"I think it's looking like a possibility but I can't say for sure. I'll find something I'm sure."

"Do you think the police should be involved?"

"Possibly but this death will mean they are stretched, so I'll keep going for a bit longer. I know from previous experience that evidence is what's needed to ensure the police can get results and make the best use of their time."

Colin reappeared with the same tray his father had used on my previous visit. He gave his father his tea and he sat next to his dad.

"Colin, do you mind if I ask you some questions?"

"Not at all," he said willingly.

"How well do you know Alicja?"

"Pretty well, I suppose." His speech was slow and considered, speaking quietly almost as if he was in a library. Unlike his parents, his accent was that of a native of Fife.

"Do you think she would be the kind of woman to take off without a word to anyone?"

"I don't think so but she may have met someone. People can do strange things when they are in love. Things that are out of character." His words carried the weight of experience behind them.

"I suppose so, but from what you know of her would that seem unlikely?"

"Yes. She seems responsible, she calls her family regularly, never causes any problems on the farm. It does seem a bit strange."

"What about Neil Bennett?"

He immediately became defensive. "What about him?"

"How did she get on with him?"

"Neil can be difficult for people who don't understand him."

"Do you understand him?"

"We served in Bosnia together." He leaned forward from his seat and looked at me with a forceful intensity. "Have you ever served in the army, Mr Campbell?"

"No, I haven't."

"There are bonds forged in war, particularly during combat, that are lifelong. You overlook the faults in people if you know they have your back, that's a trust you don't get anywhere else."

"Your loyalty is admirable. I understand your need to look after your friend but he seems to rub people the wrong way. He doesn't seem to be the best person to be a supervisor. Have you any thoughts on that?"

"What? You think you know what's best? You've met the guy and made a snap decision. That I should dump him just because he's insensitive. He stays. I think I know how best to run my own business." He sat back in his seat, his body language defensive. His father gave him a suffering look. I guessed he had started similar conversations that had produced the same results.

Bennett was like a leaking septic tank, poisoning everything around him with slow drips of his particular bile. No one thought he was violent but his attitude to the staff under his supervision showed a level of contempt that could lead him to do anything.

"What regiment did you serve with?"

"The Coldstream Guards."

"Was Bennett in a promoted post in the army?"

"No, a private, I was his corporal."

"Did he ever suffer any trauma?"

He stared at me with a greater intensity than I had ever seen before in anyone.

"As much and no more than the rest of us." His short answer spoke volumes about both Bennett and him. They had seen things, maybe had to do things that had affected them but it was the private concern of comrades in arms, there was no space for a civilian's opinions.

"Where did you serve?"

"Vitez and Sarajevo."

"Sarajevo was rough?"

"You've no idea. It would make hell look like a dream holiday resort." I could see his discomfort at the mere mention of the town.

"Has Neil ever been violent since he came out? Some people can suffer from PTSD after serving in a war zone."

"Not that I know. That PTSD is a load of crap, everybody has bad days, whether you've served or not." He was now very cold towards me. I was intruding on memories of a brotherhood that no outsider would ever understand.

"How did he end up working here? Your Dad mentioned something about him struggling with life after the army."

He glared at his father, a real sense of rage burning in his gaze.

"Neil's a simple man, life in the army was uncomplicated, he went where he was told, when he was told, to do what he was told. Without that structure, he was aimless, he had no anchor point. He told me that he couldn't cope with life outside, so I offered him a job here. I understood what he needed, the sense of order that he was lacking."

"It sounds, to me, as if giving him responsibility

over others is not the best thing. He isn't what you would call a born leader."

"I don't give a damn what you think," he said aggressively. He stood up and I thought that he might hit me but his father held him gently and seemed to break the spell.

"Right, that's fine. It was an observation, that's all."

I tried to placate him by changing the subject. "Was there anyone new around the farm in the last few weeks? Delivery men, casual workers?"

He sat down again and turned his fixed stare towards me, contempt clouding his face. "There are different people in and out all the time, it's a working farm. We get lorries delivering and picking up every day."

"Do you know if any of them showed any interest in Alicja?"

"No. Not that I know of. Is that everything? I need to get back to work."

"Yes, that's all I have to ask at the moment but I'm sure I'll be back."

"Goodbye." He stood and walked from the room. The outside door rattled as he banged it shut.

Mr Rose shook his head. "I'm sorry Mr Campbell but my son has a very large blind spot where Neil Bennett is concerned. Brothers in arms."

"That's OK, Mr Rose. It's not your fault."

"You don't think that Bennett could have hurt

the girl?" His concern was genuine, which told me that I wasn't the only one who thought that Bennett was a loose cannon.

"I don't know but his attitude to women does leave a lot to be desired. I'll keep going, something will turn up soon, I'm sure. Let's hope that your son is right, that Alicja has found someone and that she's been swept up in the moment. I'll leave you in peace."

I stood and walked out with Mr Rose saying his farewell to my back.

The Land Rover was gone from the door, my Ducati sat in isolation in the yard. I climbed on board and decided to head back to Glasgow. I would call my mother and let her know that I was going home for the night.

*

Back at my own flat in Glasgow, I left a message on my mother's voice mail. I then rang Carol to let her know I was home. I had hardly finished the sentence when she said that she would be over.

She arrived at about seven. I kissed her with an ardent, longing passion at the front door which she returned with equal ferocity.

"It's great to see you." I meant every word as the realisation dawned on me that she was now a hugely important part of my life.

"You too, handsome." Her infectious grin only added to my pleasure.

"Is the case over?" she asked.

"No. It's been slow progress so I thought I would come back for some extra clothes and, of course, to see you."

"Good answer. Tell me all about it then."

Back in the living room, I talked her through the case, including the visit to the mortuary. She listened intently, asking questions and sympathising where it was needed. It was one of the reasons that I had fallen for her so deeply, so quickly. She was an excellent listener and I loved the time we spent talking. It was like a friendship we had shared for years rather than only five months.

We ordered a pizza to share accompanied by a bottle of Chianti that I had tucked away in a cupboard.

While we were waiting for the pizza to be delivered, I booted up my Mac and read some e-mail. I also scanned the picture of Alicja with Stefania and loaded it into my phone.

When the food arrived we sat at the dining table, relaxing in each other's company. It was a comforting domestic scene that was a distraction from the exasperation at my lack of headway in the case.

Afterwards, we went to bed, entwined in each other's arms. Before long the kisses became more passionate and we found an expression for our desire in the heat of our touch.

SUNDAY 18TH APRIL, 2010

It was well after eleven the following morning before we made our way from the bedroom. I felt fully rested, a relief after some restless nights in my mother's old spare bed.

Showered and shaved, I began to make breakfast while Carol soaked in a bath. She enjoyed a bath on a Sunday morning, allowing the relaxation of the weekend to cocoon her completely, appreciating every moment away from the daily grind of life at the clothes factory.

We sat together at the dining table, savouring some croissants and coffee. Carol filled me in with the details of the end of her week. Her Uncle John was in a cheerful mood, for a change, thanks to one of his chihuahuas, Charisse. His top bitch, she had claimed a best in class at the West Of Scotland Chihuahua Club show. I still struggled to reconcile the image of John Dolan parading any dog in a show ring, never mind the smallest of all dogs.

When we were finished with breakfast, Carol offered to do the dishes.

During our discussion of the case the previous evening I had mentioned the link to Robbie Michaels and his lap dancing club. Carol suggested that maybe Alex, my ex-girlfriend who is a Detective Sergeant in the Strathclyde police force, might know someone among her colleagues in Tayside who would be able to give me some information. While Carol was busy, I picked up the phone.

My relationship with Alex had settled to a comfortable pattern again. Carol and I had attended Alex's engagement party in March, while she and Andrew had come to my 30th birthday celebration. She seemed to be genuinely pleased that Carol and I were happy together. I was equally delighted for her, as her fiancé seemed to be the ideal partner for her.

"Hello, Craig. How are you?" She was upbeat and relaxed.

"I'm good, thanks Alex. And you?"

"Working away, keeping my head down, you know, the usual. How's Carol?"

"She's fine, I've got her in the kitchen, tied to the sink, so she knows her place. Oi!" A stream of water ran down my back from the very wet dish cloth that was now resting on my head.

"That was me being reminded who the real boss is."

Alex laughed and I joined her as Carol stuck her

tongue out at me from the kitchen.

"So, is this a social call or are you looking to get yourself into more hot water?" Alex laughed again at her own little joke.

"No hot water, at least I hope not, but I'm hoping you might be able to help me."

"Is this a professional request?" The laughter was gone.

"Yes. I'm looking into the disappearance of a young woman in Fife. She's a Polish migrant worker, based just outside St Andrews. She's been gone for over a week now and I've found a possible link to a guy named Robbie Michaels in Dundee. I was hoping you might have a contact in the Tayside force and that they might be able to give me some information."

"Michaels?" Her voice rang with recognition.

"Aye, do you know him?"

"Oh yes. He's quite a lad is Robbie Michaels."

My curiosity piqued, I asked, "How do you know him?"

"He's quite the happy wanderer is Mr Michaels. He arrived in Glasgow from Liverpool about four years ago. He had caused some grief to his bosses in the Liverpool gangland, the kind that might get him badly hurt. He was sent North to work for his cousin, Jamie McIntyre, who is part of a team that work out of Darnley."

"When you say work, I take it you don't mean they are the local plumbers."

"No, definitely not. Prostitution is Mr McIntyre's racket of choice. We came across Michaels about eighteen months ago, a young prostitute was badly beaten and left under one of the bridges on the Clyde, we think she was supposedly under his wing. We knew that Michaels was guilty but before we could get the girl to testify, they got to her and she suddenly found herself in a nice new flat in the Merchant City, rent free. For some reason her memory failed her after that, must have been the altitude of her new apartment or something," she finished sarcastically.

"So how did he end up in Dundee?"

"The McIntyre clan were looking to expand their business interests. Dundee was lacking that one essential leisure attraction that all big cities need these days, a lap dancing club. The trouble with the girl meant that they wanted Michaels as far away as they could, while still being able to keep an eye on him. They sent him up to Dundee to run the club that they had just acquired a licence for."

"Has there been any indication they were involved in sex trafficking, particularly from Eastern Europe?"

"No, the girls we've come across down here are all local but that's not to say that Michaels isn't showing his own initiative. Although from what I've heard he's not big on thinking. Do you want me to check with Tayside, see what they've heard?"

"That would be great, Alex. From what I've learned there's a suggestion that he seems to prey on the young girls that come to Fife for the farm work. It's maybe a case of them getting more for lying on their back rather than breaking it in a field."

"Yeah, he would probably hire them out for a larger fee, there are creeps out there who will pay extra for the exotic, something a bit different from the poor skinny housing scheme girls that are the norm."

"Did you hear about the body found at Tentsmuir?"

"Yes, not a lot to go on so far, from what I hear and read."

"I took my client to have a look at the body but it wasn't the girl I'm looking for. Do you think Michaels could be involved in that? Is he capable of murder?"

"Judging by what he did to the girl in Glasgow, it's distinctly possible. He's a nasty piece of work and pretty thick with it. I would suggest you tell the Tayside investigative team the information you have and let them have a look at him. He'll probably be on their radar for the murder anyway."

I thought that this was a familiar response, no one thought I could look after myself. "I'll be careful, I promise."

"What makes you think that he was connected to your girl, anyway?"

"One of the last people to see her mentioned that Michaels supplied girls for parties. I was reaching for straws, but I thought it was worth a look. Information has been very thin on the ground."

"Look, I advise you to get the police to talk to him."

"Yeah, whatever you say."

"You have no intention listening to me do you? It's December all over again," she said crossly.

"Look, it's probably nothing to do with him but I have to ask."

"Jesus, you're impossible."

"There's someone else that I've got my eye on. A guy called Neil Bennett. He's ex-army but I think he might have been in some kind of trouble since he came out. He's a Fifer, so if you've got any contacts up there that could help me, I would be grateful."

"Have you an address for him?"

"No but he works at the Rose Farm and I think he lives in St Andrews. He was in the Coldstream Guards if that's any help."

"It's not a lot to go on but I'll see what I can do."

"Thanks for your help, Alex. If Tayside have got anything on Michaels, I'll leave it to them, I promise."

"Fine. I'll give a couple of colleagues a ring."

"Cheers, catch you later."

"Bye."

Carol was standing at the kitchen door. "What was that all about?"

"Just getting some information from Alex."

"I meant the last part. Are you putting yourself

in danger again?"

"No, don't be daft."

She held my gaze, trying to measure if I was telling the truth or not. She walked towards me, her stare never deviating from my eyes.

"You better be telling me the truth, I don't want to be sitting beside a hospital bed again."

"I'll be fine, honest boss."

Her face broke into a smile, "And don't you forget who the boss is, boy."

She wrapped her arms around me and kissed me.

"I better get organised and get back to Fife."

"So soon. Isn't there something else you'd rather be doing?"

"Well…"

She took my hand and led me back to the bedroom.

*

By three o'clock I was back on the road. The pleasant memories of my time with Carol still gave me an agreeable tingle.

Despite Alex's warning, I had decided to pay Michaels' club a visit. I rode the bike up the M90 to Perth and along the A90, following the course of the Tay valley to Dundee. I parked in a public car park across from the building that housed the Starlight club.

I walked across a footbridge over the bustling

road that leads to the Tay Bridge.

This part of Dundee is a strangely deserted area, a buffer between the riverside tourist attractions and the main shopping area. It was as if it had landed between two planning zones, neither one thing nor the other, as a result it had faded into insignificance.

The club is in the basement of what used to be the Tay Hotel. It is an austere building, dull grey stone, with all the warmth of a Calvinist sermon. It may have been grand when it was first built but its former glory is a long forgotten memory.

The entrance to the Starlight club was discreet: a plain red door was marked with a simple brass plaque bearing the legend Starlight Gentleman's Club. Members Only. Below the sign, a controlled entrance button and speaker.

I pressed the buzzer and waited for a reply.

"We're shut." A Dundonian accent, gruff and abrupt.

"I want to speak to Robbie Michaels."

"He's no' in."

"Ah'm Craig Campbell, ah'm fae Glesga." I hoped that exaggerating my Glaswegian accent might make him think I was someone from the McIntyre crew. It worked.

"Oh right. You better come in then."

A bleep sounded to tell me the door was unlocked. I swung the dark, heavy wood open. Behind it was a staircase going down to what must have been the basement of the old hotel. It was tastefully decorated - unfortunately the taste was Elvis Presley's Graceland circa 1974. There was a deep red carpet, the walls had a heavy flock wallpaper, its floral pattern the colour of the carpet, set against a silver background. The lighting was muted, giving the place the atmosphere of a cheap bordello, but the proprietor probably thought that it was the epitome of class and refinement.

At the bottom of the stairs was a cloakroom to the right and on the left, the entrance to the club itself. Inside, a thick set man in his early thirties stood leaning on a brush. He was almost bald, a thin crescent of black hair giving him the look of an extremely aggressive monk. He had one black eye and a sticking plaster over the other: it looked like sweeping wasn't his only duty. His head seemed to sit directly on his American footballer's shoulders. He wore a Nike T-shirt over his rotund torso, a pair of cheap jogging trousers and trainers completing the look that all the fashion world was striving for, well maybe not.

"The boss is through there."

He attempted to gesture with his head to a door at the far end of the bar, his body also had to move as there was no flexibility in his neck to allow him to use his head alone.

As I walked towards the door I took note of my surroundings. The club was lit by unforgiving yellow fluorescent bulbs, exposing the tawdry surroundings that the dazzling spotlights of night would conceal.

Despite only being a year old, the couches and chairs were stained with alcohol, at least I hoped that was what caused the mess. The carpet was the same brothel red as the stairwell but soiled by overturned drinks and the regurgitations of the over-imbibed. The stage had two poles for the dancers to perform their art, mirrors on the wall at the back reflected the scene, blue sequinned curtains protected the wings. Two middle-aged women were working: one pushing a vacuum cleaner back and forth while she danced to the private tunes playing in her earphones while the other was trying to polish a shine on to some brass fittings behind the bar. They didn't even glance in my direction as I sauntered passed.

The office door was closed, so I knocked before opening it.

Inside, a thin man with a nose like a vulture's beak sat behind a desk. His skin had a sickly pallor, his brown hair hung slackly from his skeletal skull. A poorly healed burn scar marked him like a broken necklace, tracing a ragged line from the left of his neck down into his shirt. His clothes were expensive designer label, gangsta rapper chic. All black, gold and white, it may have looked cool on Jay-Z but definitely looked ridiculous on a Scouse nobody.

The room was not much bigger than a cupboard. A row of box files lined a shelf behind Michaels' head. There was a dirty checkered linoleum covering on the floor.

"Who de fuck are you?" The accent was as Liverpudlian as the Mersey ferry. One sentence and he had pressed my buttons. I knew his history as a woman beater and any chance I would give him the benefit of the doubt was gone with five words.

"Craig Campbell, I'm a private detective."

"What?"

"Craig Campbell, I'm a private detective," I repeated, loudly as if he was deaf.

"I'm not fuckin' deaf you tosser. Who let you in me club?"

"Your man out there."

"McLaghan, git your stupid arse in here!" he bawled.

McLaghan waddled in, a sheepish look on his face.

"Whit have ah done noo?"

"You let this fucker in me club. Get him out."

"Ah thought he was a weegie."

"He is but not one of ours. Get him out."

He stepped towards me as his master had instructed.

"Look, I'm here to ask some questions and then I'll be gone." I held my hands up to show that I wasn't there to cause any problems.

"I don't give a shit, throw him out." Michaels was insistent, making a show of turning his attention to the desk, he moved some papers.

McLaghan stepped towards me once again. Using

the reflexes that had been developed at Tae Kwon Do, I aimed a biker's boot down the right shin of the obedient employee. Although it does little long-term damage, it's normally a painful and effective way to stop someone in their tracks and it was a useful technique in the circumstances.

"What the fuck!" McLaghan roared his agony as he clutched at his legs.

"Hey you, what d'you think you're up to?" Michaels stood up but there was a hesitancy about him. I reckoned he was used to other people taking orders and executing his violent intentions for him, except when the target was a woman, then he would be able to do his own dirty work.

"Answer the questions, I'll be gone and you can get back to running your little sex den."

"Who de fuck d'you think you are? This is a legitimate gentleman's club."

"Yes, I know. You can tell me all about it and how Santa, the tooth fairy and the Easter bunny are your best customers. Send the pet away and we can talk."

McLaghan had regained some of his composure and looked to his boss for further instruction. Michaels shook his head, his face fixed in fury. "Leave it. Get out."

McLaghan trotted away but not before he drew me a look that meant I wouldn't be expecting any Christmas cards from him.

"Private detective. What the fuck's dat all about?"

"At the moment it's all about a missing girl."

He was immediately defensive. "Gerl, I don't know nuttin' about a missing gerl."

"If you let me tell you a bit more, maybe you'll know something. OK if I sit?"

"No. You won't be stayin' long. You're a fuckin' prick."

"It's a character weakness but I'll get over it. Now the girl I'm looking for is called Alicja. She's Polish and I believe you have a stable of Eastern European women to call upon. Some might even say that they are call girls." I smiled but he didn't seem to be in the mood for humour.

"Call gerls? You've been watchin' too much telly mate. All my gerls werk here, at me club. There's no call gerls."

"Let's just say that I have it on good authority that you are willing to supply women to men in need of a certain kind of company."

"Yir aut'ority is talkin' shite."

"OK. Fine, whatever you say. Take a look at this picture and tell me if you've ever seen her. She's maybe friendly with one of your dancers." I put a heavy emphasis on the last word but the sarcasm sailed over the dullard's head, following the same path as much of his education I imagined. I showed him the girls' picture on my phone.

"She's on the left."

He took a cursory glance at her features. "No,

don't know her."

"You might want to take a longer look, just to be sure."

"I said I don't know her, OK. Who is she anyway?"

"Her name's Alicja Symanski and she works at the Rose Farm, near St Andrews."

As I spoke, a flicker of recognition altered his features for a brief moment.

"Do you know the farm?"

"No, why would I?"

"Your mouth says no but your face says yes."

"Change that description, you're not a prick, you're a fuckin' arsehole."

"Yeah and you're a poor put upon legitimate businessman, we all have our crosses to bear. What do you know about Rose Farm?"

I could see his reluctance but he seemed to decide that he wanted rid of me and that telling me something might be a way of achieving that. "Some of me gerls used to werk there."

"At the farm?"

"Yeah, I've got a contact on the inside. He points me towards the vulnerable ones, the shaggable ones that are a bit poorer, a bit more needier, and if I recruit dem he gets a finder's fee. I've got a few talent scouts around."

I was momentarily stunned. "How many girls work for you who used to work there?"

He shrugged. "About four or five."

"Who's this inside contact?"

"No, I'm not tellin' you that. Now ye can fuck off."

As he spoke he looked out into the main floor of the club. McLaghan was walking towards us with a baseball bat swinging menacingly from his right hand.

"'S'alright Mack, this dick's just leavin'. I'm sick of listening to his shite."

Resigned to not getting any further, I had one last dig. "Are you still beating up women, Robbie?"

"What the fuck you talkin' about now?"

"That girl you used as a punch bag in Glasgow, got any fresh punch bags in Dundee? You wouldn't want to get out of shape up here, would you?"

"Fuck off. Get this fuckin' arsehole out me club," he shouted at McLaghan.

The bouncer moved towards me and swung with the bat. It caught me on the right thigh before I could evade it. I went down clutching my leg, McLaghan aimed a couple of kicks at my ribs. He was about to add a third when Michaels interrupted him, "Dat's enough, Mack. Get him out and never let 'im in again. Understand?"

McLaghan hauled me up and dragged me to the staircase.

"Don't think ye'll ever catch me like that again. Fuck off." McLaghan's final words were filled with the bravado of a man holding a weapon.

I hobbled out of the club and back to the bike. Fortunately, my bike leathers had offered me a degree of protection from the assault and I would be spared any broken ribs but the bruises would be colourful. My thigh had less protection and smarted as a result of the impact but I hoped that it would fade quickly.

It was now five o'clock and I didn't feel up to trying to investigate any further. I felt that Michaels was hiding something but that had probably been the story of his life so far.

*

It was a painful journey to Arbroath, my ribs and thigh complained at every movement of the bike, every bump in the road.

Fortunately, my mother was out when I arrived back. Having let myself in with the key she had entrusted to me, I found the medicine cabinet, swallowed a couple of strong painkillers, rubbed on some arnica and checked the damage in the bedroom mirror. I'd live.

A renewing cup of Chiapas coffee was next on my priority list and I brewed a pot before I sat in the living room with my Macbook on my lap. I typed up my notes and enjoyed the reviving properties of the coffee. The painkillers began to work their magic and I felt a little less fragile.

I wrote notes to remind me what I needed to do to progress the case. I still had to interview some more people from the party, if I could find some who would be willing to talk to me. Doctor Barclay would have to

117

be quizzed and I still had to find a translation service that could help me with Alicja's journal. I had thought about asking Stefania but there might be something in there she didn't want me to know about.

There was also the very relevant question of the role Neil Bennett played in this. I thought he would be the one supplying Michaels with the inside information from the farm, it sounded like the kind of thing that he would get a kick out of. I wondered if he had made advances to Alicja, possibly trying to use his position as leverage over her. Her rejection of him would have upset his ego. It could conceivably have led to her disappearance and all that may have followed.

An hour after I had arrived, Mum came in. She had been visiting a friend in Montrose for the afternoon and was flushed red by spending time in the sun. She would have given me a hard time if I had come home burnt like that but I knew better than to comment.

She cooked some pasta bolognese for us while she told me about her afternoon. I filled her in on my visit to the club, deliberately omitting my less than dignified exit.

As we chatted, she made a sudden exclamation. "Oh, I was wondering if you could do me a favour?"

"What's that then?"

"Mrs Gilbert was in this morning, before I went to Montrose. She was saying that her cat's gone missing, I said I'd ask you to have a look." She smiled sheepishly, knowing how much I avoided doing anything like that when I was working.

"You don't have to do much but it would mean a lot to her if you gave it a try."

I sighed, "OK, is she far away?"

"No, just round the corner."

"Right, let me get my cat detection kit." I said with a degree of sarcasm.

"Sorry."

"If you weren't my mother..." I smiled to show that I wasn't too angry.

We were ready within five minutes after we had finished dinner. Mother led me round to Mrs Gilbert's house. It was a substantial Victorian semi-detached, built with the red sandstone that was commonly used around the town. Even the ancient Arbroath Abbey was built of a very similar material.

Mrs Gilbert opened the door to us. Despite her being in her late sixties, her hair was still dark brown, peppered with a little grey. She wore an apron with a selection of fruits printed on it. The garment protected a brown tweed skirt. Her pale yellow sweater looked expensive, a fine lambswool or even cashmere. She was also wearing a pair of bright yellow rubber gloves, which had soap suds still clinging to them.

"Oh sorry, you've caught me in the middle of the dishes. Come in, come in." She gestured with the gloves, causing a ball of foam to detach from the glove and land on my jeans.

"Sorry, I'm all flustered since my Sandy disappeared. I'm through here."

We followed her through to her kitchen at the back of the house. It was furnished with traditional looking but obviously new cupboards. A solid range-style cooker which was painted teal blue occupied one wall and a small kitchen table was placed against one of the other walls. Three chairs surrounded the table and she invited us to sit while she removed her gloves and began to wipe the sink. She wiped quickly but conscientiously, making sure she had covered every bit of the surface.

"Thanks for coming, Craig. I hope you don't mind but I'm so worried about my poor Sandy, he's never been away this long." She removed the apron as she spoke and placed it on a hook behind the kitchen door. She fussed around putting dishes in cupboards and straightening storage jars that were a centimetre out of alignment.

"When did you last see him?" I asked.

"Friday night. He normally comes back about ten from his travels. He doesn't stay out at night."

While Mrs Gilbert finished her domestic tasks, I thought I could hear a scraping noise.

"Did anyone hear that?"

"What?" my mother asked.

"That noise."

Everyone was silent and still for a few seconds before I heard the sound again. There was a distinct scratching coming from below our feet.

My mother was the first to react. I wondered if Mrs Gilbert's had problems with her hearing, it might explain why she hadn't heard the cat. "I heard it, it's coming from under the floor boards."

"What is it? Do you think it could be Sandy?" Mrs Gilbert's voice rose with hope.

The kitchen floor boards, solid oak by the look of them, were bare of any covering so it would be a simple task to lift a couple to investigate.

"Do you have a hammer and chisel, Mrs Gilbert?"

"I'm sure there'll be something in the garage. I haven't touched anything since my William passed."

"I'll take a look."

She handed me the key and I went through the back door to the large garden. The flowers and lawn reflected a patience and skill for gardening that I could only admire.

The rusting hinges of the black wooden garage doors yielded after a little persuasion. The smell of wood shavings, oil and dust engulfed me as I walked in. With the doors wide open it was easy to see the well-organised tools and work benches. The back wall was mainly wood-working tools including a lathe. At one side there were spanners and other tools I recognised as being for working on engines although I wouldn't have been able to use them. The impression I got from this masculine hideaway was of a skilled and tidy man, a man who took pride in his abilities and joy from his hobbies. I wondered how he would have felt about the thin coating of dust that had settled over his little dominion.

I found a large chisel on a shelf, part of a full set that were organised according to their size, every blade shining like new. There were two hammers hanging from hooks, a big claw hammer and a smaller pin hammer. I chose the larger of the two and walked back across the garden to the house.

When I returned to the kitchen, my mother was comforting Mrs Gilbert, who was crying tears of joy or anxiety, or both, it was difficult to know.

I started to ease the chisel in to a joint on one of the boards close to the back door. I tapped the handle gently with the hammer, trying not to split the wood.

While I worked I asked Mrs Gilbert to get me a torch. She rumbled in one of the kitchen drawers and handed me a fairly large light. After some patient work, three boards were lifted and I shone the torch into the space beneath the floor. A pair of eyes reflected green light back at me.

"I think he's there but there's something in the way, I'll see if I can get it out."

I reached into the space and was greeted by a vicious hiss from the visibly overwrought cat. My ribs and thigh were throbbing in agony as I stretched every sinew to reach the blockage. Finally, I managed to get a grip on it and slid it towards the gap in the boards. It was a rough wooden box, about two feet long, a foot wide and nine inches deep. When I had removed it the cat ran and leapt out of the space I had created, swiping an ungrateful claw and spitting violently at me as he passed.

"Sandy, come to mum." Mrs Gilbert's tears were drying on her happily grinning face. The cat walked towards her arrogantly, tail in the air, then miaowed loudly and went to stand next to a cupboard.

"Oh, ma poor boy. Are you hungry? How did you get under there, you silly cat? Were you chasing mice again? You naughty boy." Mrs Gilbert fussed around, getting the cat food out of the cupboard and putting into a dish while Sandy circled her legs, rubbing his owner and purring loudly.

She then addressed my mother and me. "He must have got in through one of the old vents. I wonder why he didn't miaow. Not that it matters, thank you Craig."

"You're welcome."

While the joyful reunion continued, I began to try to prise the lid of the small box open. The wood looked like it had come from an old orange crate or a tea chest. I eased each of the eight nails out and the lid fell off.

My mother had joined me to see what treasures the box contained but we both gasped when the contents were revealed.

Inside the improvised coffin was the skeleton of a baby. There were remnants of some cloth that might have been silk, a dress or a christening robe was my first impression. The little body was lying with its arms crossed, resting in crumpled pieces of aged newspapers. I noticed the date on one of the pages read 12th August, 1960.

Mrs Gilbert had joined us to see what had provoked our reaction.

"Oh, oh dear." She had her hand to her mouth while my mother stood beside her, large teardrops silently slid down Mum's face as she contemplated the tiny casket.

No one said a word for a couple of minutes, each of us too stunned to comment on my tragic find, a short life stilled before it had even really started.

I managed to compose myself and realised I had to do something. "We need to call the police."

Mrs Gilbert nodded as if she was in a daze as my mother said, "Yes, of course, son. You're right."

I walked out of the kitchen into the hall and looked up the number for the local police in Arbroath on my phone. The phone rang twice before a voice said, "Tayside Police, Arbroath station, Sergeant Yates speaking." He sounded bored.

"Good evening, Sergeant. I'd like to report a body."

His boredom was dispelled quickly as he replied, "Right, sir. Can you give me the details?"

I explained the saga of the cat, how I found the skeleton and gave him Mrs Gilbert's address.

"Sir, I'm not trying to be smart but are you sure

it's real? It's not a prop or some medical study aid?"

"I can't be one hundred percent sure but the bones certainly look real and there are some remnants of clothing."

"OK, we'll have someone come straight round."

My mother led Mrs Gilbert through to the front room while I made them both a sweet cup of tea to help to counteract the shock.

Twenty minutes later a marked police car drew up outside the house and two uniformed officers got out.

I greeted them at the door and led them into the room where my mother was talking with Mrs Gilbert.

The policemen introduced themselves as Constables Kerrigan and Watson. Constable Kerrigan, who was the younger of the two, asked Mrs Gilbert some questions about how long she had been in the house, who owned it previously and a few other details. Meanwhile Watson asked if he could see the skeleton.

I preceded him into the kitchen and revealed my find.

He took out his notebook and pen. I reckoned him to be in his early thirties, athletic with broad shoulders. He had black hair on top of his long head. He had an intense gaze which was slightly unnerving and would prove useful to him if he ever became a detective.

"Can you tell me what happened, sir?"

"Please, call me Craig."

"Well Craig, what's the story?"

I repeated the tale I had already given the sergeant on the phone. Constable Watson nodded and made positive noises, as I described the circumstances of the discovery of the grisly secret of the house.

"And what do you do for a living?"

"I'm a private investigator and insurance claims inspector."

He glanced up from his notebook. A cynical smirk passed across his face before it returned to the professionally neutral expression that he had previously.

He finished taking my details before he stated, "C.I.D. will have to take a look and the scene of crime guys might want to pay a visit as well."

"Yes, I understand."

We walked back through to the front room and Mrs Gilbert, who was still visibly shaken. Constable Watson repeated to her what the police were going to do, as she was consoled by my mother. Mum said she would stay with her that night to keep her company.

About an hour later another car pulled up outside the house. A man and a woman walked up the path and I met them at the door. They were both detectives, the woman was Detective Inspector Logan and her colleague was introduced as Detective Constable Thomas.

I spent another half hour answering their questions before I asked to be excused. I left them my card with my mobile number, they thanked me for my help and I walked back with Mum to her flat. She was going to get some overnight things for her stay with Mrs Gilbert.

"Do you think the baby was murdered?" She began when we had cleared the gate outside Mrs Gilbert's house.

"I don't know, Mum."

"I wonder what happened. Who could do that to a child?"

"I don't know, Mum."

She stopped and looked at me intently. "Are you going to investigate?"

"That's why I called the police, Mum. It's got nothing to do with me."

"They probably won't do much."

"The body will be taken to the mortuary, if someone killed the baby, it's possible that the pathologists might find out for sure. Hopefully they'll be able to discover what happened and if there's a crime been committed they'll investigate. Maybe it was too long ago to know how the baby died and it'll be a tragic incident from the past. I'm sure they'll try and trace any relatives no matter what they do or don't find."

"But what if there's no relatives, what happens to the body?"

"I'd imagine it'll be the council's responsibility."

"Oh poor wee thing. Not even a decent burial." She walked on, internalising her thoughts until we reached the flat.

"I've decided to find out about that baby."

I almost groaned. "Mum, leave it to the police." The irony struck home, me telling anyone to leave it to the police.

"No. I'm going to find out more about who lived in that house before Mrs Gilbert, find anyone who knows about the baby. If we can't, we need to organise a decent burial for the poor wee lamb." Her tone of voice meant that she was set and not ready to compromise, so I decided it would better to let her go ahead. I knew that she could be very stubborn once her mind was made up, probably the genetic source of my own obstinacy.

"Fine, Mum."

She smiled and patted my cheek. She busied herself getting pyjamas, a change of clothes and her overnight bag. We said goodnight and she headed off back to her friend's house.

Exhausted and in considerable pain, my only concern was another cup of coffee and another shot of painkillers.

I turned on the T.V. and flicked through the channels before finding a nature programme about jaguars. I watched it without absorbing any information, my mind now filled with two separate bodies as well as the missing Alicja. When the programme finished, I called Carol.

"Hi gorgeous."

"Hello yourself, how are you? Not too exhausted

from your exertions of last night and this morning, I hope." I could hear the mischievous smile that I was sure was on her face.

"Exhausted, yes. But that's not the reason."

"Got someone else exerting you?" she asked with mock jealousy.

"No. I was hunting a cat and got more than I bargained for."

"A cat?"

"Mum had me helping one of her friends. The cat was under the floorboards but that wasn't all I found. There was a baby's skeleton in a box."

"You're kidding!"

"'Fraid not. The police are round at Mrs Gilbert's place now."

"That's terrible Craig."

"Mother's determined to investigate and find out more about the baby and then organise a funeral."

"The detection gene must run in your family."

I smiled, "Aye, I reckon you're right."

We talked some more, I told her the rest of my day, missing out my involuntary stint as a football for McLaghan. What she didn't know wouldn't harm me.

I went to bed after the phone call ended. I was asleep within minutes, so exhausted not even my complaining, creaking ribs could keep me awake.

MONDAY 19TH APRIL, 2010

The sun had surrendered to the clouds again on the Monday morning. The view of the sea from Mum's spare bedroom was masked by the drizzling rain, which cast a depressing air over the seaside town.

I dressed gingerly, my movements restricted by my injured ribs and throbbing thigh, which both felt stiff after a night in bed.

I had probably come on too strong with Michaels but there was something about him that had immediately got under my skin.

After another two capsules of Ibuprofen, I made some toast and some coffee. Mum was still round at Mrs Gilbert's, so I didn't have to listen to her concerns about my lack of appetite in the morning.

Breakfast over, I picked up the phone.

"Hi Hero, it's Craig Campbell."

"Oh, hi Craig. How are you?"

"I'm fine, thanks. Hero, I need to talk to some of the other guests who attended the party. Is there any chance you could arrange something?"

"Yeah, I'll see what I can do. What about this afternoon?" He sounded eager to help.

"Sounds good, I'll be in St Andrews anyway."

"I'll give you a ring to let you know where and when."

"Cheers, thanks."

After hanging up, I looked up the number of the university. I was going to go direct to Barclay but I thought it might be better to be a bit circumspect.

"Good morning, St Andrews University, John speaking, how may I help you?"

"Good morning, John. I was wondering if it would be possible to speak to Doctor Barclay."

"One moment, please." There was a brief burst of Haydn before he returned. "Is it Doctor Roger Barclay you're looking for?"

"That's right."

"I'll put you through to the school of biology."

Haydn's trumpet concerto once again filled my ear as I waited.

A woman answered. "St Andrews University, school of biology, Elizabeth speaking, how may I help you?"

"Hello, I'd like to speak to Doctor Barclay, please."

"I'm sorry the Doctor's in a meeting at the

moment. Can I take a message?"

"Do you know if he's free at any point today?"

There was a brief pause as she consulted the Doctor's calendar for the day. "He's got a lecture this afternoon at three, so he should be available in his office from about half one to half two."

"That's great, can you leave a message and tell him that Craig Campbell will be visiting."

"Craig Campbell. Certainly."

"Where is the Doctor's office?"

"It's down near the East Sands, in the Ocean Institute building. Ask at reception and they'll point you in the right direction."

"Thank you."

My afternoon was beginning to take shape.

I texted Rupert Haines to see if he had managed to get the details of the escort service. The reply was just a number, no greeting. His public school didn't stretch to lessons in manners by the look of it.

I sat down with the laptop again and played some Bob Dylan as an accompaniment to my work. The times they were a changin' according to Bob but there still seemed to be the same number of junk e-mails to be dealt with. There was a ton of them to be sifted through, the vast majority of which were condemned to the trash folder. Li had sent me a cheeky e-mail; glad of the momentary diversion, I replied in kind. I had seen less of Li since Carol arrived in my life but he understood, there was still the Thursday night quiz team, so it wasn't too bad.

There was a mail with a couple of follow up questions from an insurance firm about an injury claim that I could leave until I was back in Glasgow.

I was about to get ready to travel back across into the Kingdom, when my phone trilled. It was Alex.

"Hi, Alex."

"Good morning, Craig."

"What have you got for me?"

"I spoke to a guy I met at Tulliallan when we were training together. Henry Shaw, he's a DI based in Dundee. I asked him about Michaels, he is definitely on their radar with regard to vice but there doesn't seem to be any indication that sex trafficking is involved."

"Yeah, I got that impression when I spoke to him."

Her voice raised an octave, "You what?"

"I paid him a visit yesterday. He told me that there were talent scouts, as he put it, that would help him find girls from the local farms."

"What did I say? Are you really as thick as you seem to be? Michaels is connected to some seriously dangerous people. The kind of people who won't hesitate to make you disappear in a very painful way. Did December's taste of what can happen have no effect on you?" She communicated her in anger in a single burst of words without pausing for a breath.

I calmly asserted my position. "Look, I've got to

try and find this girl. I've not got a lot to go on. I'm trying to find something concrete that might help me and as flimsy as the link might have been, I had to see if he knew her."

"And did he?"

"He said no but he does have someone working at the Rose Farm. I don't think she worked for him but there was definitely a connection."

"I told Henry what you told me and they'll take a closer look at him. They can help the guys in Fife with the murder, the two forces work closely as it is."

"What about Bennett? Has he got a record?"

"If it's the same guy, he's had a couple of fines for drunk and disorderly and a suspended sentence for an affray about eight years ago but that's it."

"That must have been when Rose took him on. I was hoping that there would be more. I just need to keep digging, I suppose."

"Craig, for your own sake, you have to stop. Leave it to the professionals."

Angered by her patronising tone and at my own lack of progress, I vented my frustration at her. "Where were the professionals when Rory Kilpatrick was murdered? If they'd done their job properly back then, Mrs Capaldi might still be alive. I can look after myself and I'll do what I need to."

"Fine." She said abruptly and hung up on me. I immediately regretted my unconsidered response. I didn't want to mess up a relationship that had only got on to an even footing again. I thought about calling her back but decided that maybe giving her some breathing space would be a better idea.

I placed it at the back of my mind as I continued my preparations for the afternoon ahead.

*

I arrived in St Andrews at around mid-day and found that Hero had tried to call me during my journey.

I called him back and he told me to meet him at the flat at 12:30, which gave me about half an hour to spare and I decided to walk around the town. I hoped that it might help me to clear my head.

I set off along North Street and it lead me to memory lane. I passed the Chapel of St Salvator, the 15th Century church that forms one side of the main university quad.

A couple of hundred metres further down the New Picture House stands as a place of personal nostalgia. I had first watched The Jungle Book movie inside its classic cinema walls. Although it now offered more than one viewing screen, the main hall still reflected a time when Hollywood was king and television an expensive luxury.

With every step along the broad street the accents and language also changed: from Tennessee to Tokyo, from London to Lisbon, as if the sounds transported me to somewhere different on the planet as I progressed.

Looking at the tourists and their surroundings, I found it hard to believe that this genteel town is a place that has seen bitter bloodshed, martyrdom and all the deprivations of a besieged settlement. Religious battles were fought here as the reformation swept across Scotland. Around the town there are plaques commemorating both Protestant and Catholic martyrs, the blood of religious schism absorbed into the very paving stones of the historic streets. The division they recall still resonates and creates problems in certain parts of the country.

St Andrews is a very different place now, it represents two things, education and golf. The oldest university in Scotland carries almost the same gravitas and allure for foreign students as Oxford and Cambridge. There is a pride in the long history that the students become part of, no matter where in the world they hail from.

At the west end of North Street is Golf Links, the street that leads to the world's first golf course. The Royal and Ancient Golf Club of St Andrews is the most precious treasure of the golfing world: the great players revere it as the Holy Grail. To win at St Andrews is to write your name in history.

Golf is everywhere, from shops to galleries, in the bars and restaurants. The ancient game is the lifeblood of the modern town.

On the last green of the course, a group of players were holing out as I walked past, American accents congratulating each other on a well-played round. There would be tales and anecdotes for the bar and of course, an exaggerated version for when they returned home.

I stood and watched some Asian golfing tourists, in awe of their surroundings as they nervously teed up and hit their first drive to the wide and welcoming fairway that is shared by the Old Course's first and eighteenth holes. I always feel that first drive is like an invitation from a spider to enter her web, a tender embrace before she catches you in her trap. The Old Course can be a timid old girl when there is no wind, but in St Andrews, wind is almost guaranteed. When the gales blow in from the North Sea she becomes the femme fatale, an unrelenting and unsympathetic destroyer of a golfer's heart.

As I crossed from the golf course towards the West Sands a jet roared overhead and I watched it as it pulled round to land at RAF Leuchars on the opposite side of the Eden estuary. The noise was a frequent distraction to the golfers and formed a backdrop to any visit to the area.

The beach added another layer of nostalgic moments. Memories of building castles and flying kites, of kicking a ball and braving the cold waters by paddling up to my knees. It was busy with people creating their own moments to reminisce about. I envied their carefree day, wishing that I could throw off my cares and join them.

I strolled back into the heart of town absorbing the cosmopolitan atmosphere and ignoring the very

Scottish drizzle that had settled on the venerable place.

I spent some time looking at books in the charity shops that are never far from any student community. I bought a copy of Use Of Weapons by Fife's own Iain M. Banks. It replaced my much-loved and tattered version that had survived since my university days.

By the time I was finished my literary browsing it was time to put my past behind me. It was time to concentrate on the here and now, it was time to find Alicja.

*

Hero gave me a broad smile of welcome when he opened the door. He was wearing a scarlet turban and a Marilyn Manson T-shirt that looked terrifying.

"Come in, come in. I've managed to get four people who were at the party, they'll do what they can to help."

"Cheers."

The living room was tidier than on my last visit. Whether the detritus of student life had been secreted away into cupboards or dumped in other rooms, I wasn't sure, but it somehow seemed like a more mature room than on my previous visit.

Gerard was sitting in the rickety chair. He stood to shake my hand in a stiff and formal way, like we were about to begin a business meeting.

"Good to see you again, Mr Campbell." He indicated the seat that he had vacated.

"Thank you and it's good to see you, Gerard."

On the shabby sofa sat two women, who looked as uncomfortable as I had been on my previous visit as their backs were turned crooked by the couch. Each arm of the sofa was also occupied, one by another girl and a young man rested against other.

Hero began the introductions. "Guys, this is Craig Campbell, he's the private detective that's looking for the girl I was telling you about."

He then indicated from left to right along the couch. "This is Shelley, Alison, Marion and Kyle."

"Thanks for coming folks, I appreciate this. I don't know how much Hero's told you but basically I'm looking for a girl called Alicja Symanski who was last seen in this flat at Gerard's party. Anything you can remember about her or anything you noticed that night could be crucial in helping me to find her safe and well." I hoped that my speech would encourage them to aid me in my search.

I reached for my phone, found the picture of the two girls and passed it to Shelley with the usual speech about who was who in the picture.

Shelley was the girl on the precarious perch. She was thin, slightly bookish looking with round John Lennon-style spectacles. Behind the glasses her eyes were emerald green, alive with intelligence. Her hair was black and cascaded nearly all the way to her waist. Her face gave me an impression of wisdom beyond her relatively tender years. The clothes she wore were a defiant statement of individuality, an eclectic mixture of colours and styles, none of them designed to be together.

She held the phone at arm's length as she considered the girls' faces. It was a gesture that was reminiscent of my mother reading the newspaper, a strange habit for a young person to have, she may have problem with her eyes but it seemed contrived, a learned behaviour. I thought it was possible that she had been raised by an elderly relative. She passed the print on to Alison.

Alison was a very different character, her body was a series of pillowing rolls of fat. On top was a round head with a baby's cherubic countenance. Her hair was a fiery red and dark blue eyes peered out from below her fringe. Her clothes were more conservative than her friend's choice. A simple blue St Andrews Uni sweat shirt and a pair of black trousers. She looked nervous and discomfited at being involved in my investigation.

While Alison studied the picture, Shelley had finished her ruminations. "I seem to remember seeing her with one of the English guys, Rupert Haines, I think it was. She seemed to be quite happy when I saw her." Her accent was American, somewhere around Boston I guessed.

"Yes, I remember her with him. They seemed like, quite cosy." Alison added. She was definitely from the West Coast of Scotland.

"He said that he couldn't remember very much about her, he even suggested she might have been with an escort agency," I stated.

Shelley laughed. "That doesn't surprise me. You need to forgive Haines, he can't help being an asshole, he was born with a silver spoon in his mouth that fed him bullshit. No offence intended, Gerard."

I turned to look at Gerard who was standing in the frame of the kitchen door with a large grin on his face. "None taken," he said with some relish as he enjoyed the attack on his long-time tormentor.

The phone had by this time been passed to Marion. She was a bit older than the others, I pictured her as a mature student, or maybe she was doing some post-graduate studies. She was in her mid-twenties, broad shouldered, with the athletic build of a rower or a participant in some other muscular sport. She had an attractive face framed by brown shoulder-length hair. Her eyes were narrow and she seemed to be peering intently at whatever she looked at. She was dressed in jeans and a blue, black and white checked shirt. A silver cross dangled from a delicate necklace.

"I'm sure she arrived with Haines." Marion's voice was deep and her accent showed her to be a refined, educated Scot; any rough trace of which region of Scotland had been filed away by her upbringing and schooling.

I was surprised at what she said. "She arrived with him?"

"Yes. I opened the door to them. I was on my

way upstairs when the they knocked on the door. Of course they might just have met on the doorstep but they certainly seemed friendly."

Kyle was the next to add his opinion. "But you know what Haines is like, he thinks that he's God's gift. He'll try to shag any girl that says hello to him. He could have met her in the street and thought he could get into her knickers before they even got to the party. He's a twat."

Kyle was weedy, his superman T-shirt hung loosely on his slender frame, Clark Kent on the Atkins diet. His eyes, diminutive dots behind thick spectacles, shifted nervously between me and a spot somewhere over my right shoulder. He looked like a geek and his high squeaky voice did nothing to disavow that impression.

"I know, he's a major lecher. You feel him undressing you with his eyes every time he looks at you." This came from Marion.

"He's been like that since he was at our school," Gerard confirmed, contributing to the character assassination of Rupert while savouring every observation.

"Do you think Haines was having a relationship with Alicja?" I threw the question out to the company.

"He doesn't have relationships, he has conquests. He's sowing his wild student oats before Mummy and Daddy make him settle down with a brood mare." Marion's tone was steeped in disdain.

The others laughed. "Yes, I can see the breeder's note now, by the Earl of Sleaze out of Lady Toffingham, a fine filly." Shelley commented. This caused further laughter, I had to try to get them to focus again.

"Was there anyone at the party that made you think they were up to no good? Someone that you didn't think should be there, someone different from the people you would have expected to see." I was hoping that one of them would respond positively but it proved to be a vain hope.

The hilarity subsided. Kyle was the first to speak. "It's so hard to say. The place was mobbed and there seemed to be strangers in every room. The whole Facebook announcement thing meant there were far too many in the house. That's why it spilled out of the attic room onto the roof."

"There were definitely strangers but I wouldn't say there were any that I thought might cause any trouble," said Marion. "You normally get a sense of these things at a party. Do you know what I mean?"

"What about Eastern European girls? Were there a lot of them?" I asked.

Alison answered for the group. "There were a few, but, like, there always are. There are so many, like, migrant workers and we have a large, like, Polish contingent among the student body so it's not that surprising."

"Did you see Alicja with anyone else during the party? Someone that she spent any amount of time with?"

Shelley was the next to contribute. "I think there was another girl, possibly Eastern European. I saw them talking together a couple of times but it might just have been they met at the party."

"Did anyone see Alicja after the party?"

The all shook their head and said no.

"OK, thanks. You've been a big help."

Alison then said, "I've got some, like, photos up on my Facebook page. They might, like, have something in them."

I hoped my irritation at the creeping misuse of the word "like" was not too evident on my face.

"That's great, can you e-mail me a link and I'll check them out tonight." I gave each of them my card and asked them to get in touch if they had any further information.

I thanked everyone for their help and left them to continue to gossip about Haines.

My next stop was Doctor Barclay. I wasn't looking forward to challenging a man who had so much to lose, I couldn't be sure how he would react but it was necessary if I was going to get closer to finding out what had happened to Alicja that night.

*

I walked in the spitting rain towards the East Sands beach and the building that houses the Scottish Oceans Institute. A number of departments are involved in the study of the oceans around Scotland

and across the world, including, of course, the school of biology.

The building is constructed of a coral pink breezeblock that certainly makes it distinctive if not very attractive. As I approached the front entrance, which was to the left of the building, a rubber dinghy emerged from a shuttered portal at the opposite end. The door looked like it belonged on a domestic garage. There were three people in wet suits manoeuvring the boat, which rested on a rig designed to be towed by a car. They swung it into position and began to push it down towards the beach and from there out to meet a much larger research vessel that was at anchor in the bay.

Inside the main public door there was a small reception area. A middle-aged man sat behind the desk. He was dressed in a white shirt with the logo of a security firm sewn on a patch on the breast pocket. . He had glasses resting on the end of his nose, and he cast an annoyed glance at me over the top of them.

"Can I help you?"

"Yes, I'd like to speak to Doctor Barclay, please."

"Is he expecting you?"

"I called earlier."

"If you could fill in this pass, sir, I'll give him a call. Can I say who it is calling?"

"Craig Campbell."

While I completed the details on the form, I listened to the guard's half of the conversation.

"Doctor Barclay is wondering what it is you want to speak to him about."

"It's a personal matter regarding a mutual friend, Stefania Nowakowski." I thought that would provoke a response.

The conversation continued for a short time before the man said, "If you take a seat, Doctor Barclay will be down shortly." Before I stepped away from the desk, he handed me a security pass in a clear plastic envelope that had a clip to attach it to my clothes.

I sat in a low chair while the man at reception returned to typing on a computer. I waited ten minutes before the lift door opened and a silver-haired man came towards me.

I reckoned he was in his early fifties, his hair styled for a much younger man. His face was tanned, grey-blue eyes shone brightly in contrast to his sallow skin. He was dressed as if he'd walked out of a Gap advert. A navy blue and white T-shirt, a beige cotton pullover, stone-coloured chinos and brown slip-on loafers gave off the air of stylish youth that I felt sure he was trying to project.

He cracked an unenthusiastic, bleach-white smile at me as he offered his hand. "Mr Campbell, shall we go up?"

I followed him back to the elevator and we rode to the top floor of the complex. He didn't say a word until we were in his office and the door was securely shut behind us.

The office was styled with a simple, modern functionality. White walls covered in graphs, an oceanographic map of the Earth, photographs of various species of seals and one of a walrus. The furniture was comprised of a standard maple-coloured desk with a comfortable blue leather desk chair for the tenant, blue cloth covered maple chairs for visitors. On the desk was a laptop, a monitor and a family picture of Barclay, his wife and two lads in their early twenties, the very epitome of what advertisers would like us to believe is modern familial bliss.

The most striking feature of the room was the window, and the stunning view it offered over St Andrews Bay and beyond out towards the North-East coast of Scotland.

"What do you want?" the fake smile was gone, replaced by the concerned gaze of a man who had been caught in a lie. I needed to chip away at him to find if there was more than an affair for him to feel guilty about.

"I'm a private detective. I've been asked to look for Alicja Symanski: she hasn't been seen since a week past on Saturday." It was a simple statement, nothing in it to spook him too much, I thought.

"Never heard of her." The answer was immediate, almost believable, but his eyes betrayed his lie.

"Oh, I know you have. Just like I know that you've been doing a bit of non-curricular biological study with Stefania Nowakowski. Probably better if you tell me the truth and it'll make things go a lot quicker. I would hate to have to ask the police to take an interest, they can be so nosy, so clumsy as they dig into the darker corners of people's personal lives. They lift the rocks and all the scandalous secrets come scurrying out into the light. You never know who might find about what you've been up to."

"This is blackmail, it's outrageous." He seemed to inflate with rage.

"Get down off your high horse, Casanova. You lost the right to be indignant when you started an affair with a girl young enough to be your daughter."

He shrunk back into the leather upholstery and gave me a defiant look.

"What does it matter? It's got nothing to do with that friend of hers." He tried to maintain his composure.

"That's for me to decide, or would you rather it be decided in a police interview room?"

"OK. OK. I met Stefania about three months ago. I was out at the pub with some friends for a colleague's birthday. She was there with Alicja and some of her other friends.

"She was interesting, she's got her own view of the world, her own way of portraying herself. She's different from the arrogant students I meet every day. She doesn't think she knows everything, she wants to discover new things. I must confess I have a weakness for a pretty face, particularly one that seems to be interested in me. We started chatting and there was a connection between us. Of course I was attracted to her physically but it was more than that."

I didn't let him fool himself too much. "And she massaged your ego, your need to be thought of as young and attractive. Did you start the affair that night?"

"No, I arranged to meet her on her own. We went out to a restaurant in Edinburgh, away from the prying eyes of the town and gown set. We stayed in a hotel overnight. I've been with her once or twice a week ever since, up until that Saturday."

"What happened that night?"

"Stefania phoned about seven thirty: I had just finished dinner with my wife. I was shocked when I looked at my phone and realised it was her, she knew never to phone me at home. I was furious, I made an excuse to my wife about a problem at work. The boat's out in all weathers, all year round, so I don't think my wife suspected anything." He gestured to the vessel at anchor in the bay.

"I told Stefania that she shouldn't have told anyone but she said that Alicja had guessed. I thought we had been discreet but I suppose they've been friends for a long time. I said that I would speak to Alicja to sort it out. Stefania was upset and she told me that she wasn't going to go the party.

I called Alicja and told her I would meet her in North Street, close to the porter's lodge, at about eleven o'clock. She said that she would be there. She

149

harped on about how she wanted me to stop seeing Stefania and that I was to stop lying to her friend. She's a self-righteous little cow." His demeanour cracked, the briefest of glimpses at a man with a dangerous temper.

"Were you lying to Stefania, about leaving your wife, I mean?"

The facade was back. "What do you think? These young women can't seem to separate sex from romantic love, so I spun her a tale.

Anyway, I went in to town, we live in Craigtoun. I waited twenty minutes but she never showed. I swear I didn't see her."

"What did you say to Stefania?"

"I called her the next day and told her it was over, that I couldn't take the risk of my wife finding out."

"She told me that you told her you hadn't spoken to Alicja."

"She's mistaken, I told her that I hadn't seen her after the phone call. It's all over now, anyway."

"Maybe for you, Doctor, but there's still a young woman missing."

He placed his hands on the desk in a gesture that seemed to indicate that our meeting was over, the end of another chapter in his life, time for him to move on.

I took an educated guess. "I take it she wasn't the first."

He looked at me, a genuine smile curving his lips.

"You've got to stay young, Mr Campbell."

"Maybe you should think about her being the last. You don't know what you might get caught up in and she probably deserves better." I pointed to the family photo.

"That's my business, Mr Campbell. I'm a big boy, I can look after myself."

"I'm sure you are, just a big boy. I'll say goodbye for now but if I find you're lying to me, I'll be back and I might bring some friends in uniform with some big heavy boots."

He looked non-plussed by my barbs, water off the preening drake's back.

I got to my feet and left the office without even a hand shake or a farewell.

My walk back to the bike was filled with thoughts of the amorous Peter Pan. Women were mere toys to be played with until the novelty wore off and then they were discarded like yesterday's yo-yo. There were millions of men just like him across the globe, men who believed the fountain of youth could only be found between the legs of another woman. Men who would realise too late that there was no water of life, no secret to eternal youth, there was only a life of limited time, one chance that should be spent with people you love and who love you.

Although I believed his story up to a point, there was still something he wasn't telling me and I was determined to find out what that was.

*

I spent the rest of the afternoon back at my Mum's house. The pain of the beating I had taken had increased during the day and I was in need of some recuperation and another dose of painkillers. I was acutely aware that in terms of the case I was wasting time but I knew I wouldn't be able to function properly if I didn't give my body some proper rest.

After swallowing another couple of paracetamol, I managed to sleep for a couple of hours and was up in time to make dinner for both of us. Within the limited ingredients in my Mum's cupboards, I found enough to make a passable cottage pie. I suppose it was just mince and tatties by another name but I felt that I had achieved something.

Despite being retired, my mother has a busier life now than when she was working. Monday was one of her volunteer days, working in the British Heart Foundation's shop in Arbroath. She liked to give something back and it meant she got to talk to lots of people. My Mum likes to talk.

She arrived home at five thirty and was pleased to see that the meal was ready.

"How was your day?" I asked.

"Very interesting. I've been doing a bit of investigative work myself, about the baby," she said excitedly.

I internalised a sigh. "I thought you were volunteering today."

"I called Theresa and there were three of them in today. When she heard what I was doing she said I could take the day off. She was very interested."

"I'm sure she was. Did your detective work turn up anything interesting?"

"Yes, quite a bit. Mrs Gilbert and I spent the day talking to neighbours and checking the local church records. We were like Miss Marple and Hetty Wainthropp."

I couldn't help but grin at the thought of the world's oldest detective duo, driving the streets of Arbroath with their handbags and tea flasks at the ready. Holmes and Watson with floral dresses, sciatica and permanent waves.

"We started at Miss Finnan's house, three doors down from Mrs Gilbert's. She's been in that house since she was a little girl. She lived with her Mum and Dad until they passed away. She's in her eighties now and she told us that the family in that house before Mrs Gilbert were called Shields. There were two children, one boy and a girl. The lad was killed in an accident when he was fifteen. The girl, Bella was her name, she also died young but Miss Finnan couldn't remember the details of what had happened. She told us that we should speak to Mrs Macintyre, who lives in number 43. Well, Mrs Macintyre's mother was friendly with the Shields." She was now in full gossip mode, words flying out with machine-gun rapidity.

"Did you speak to Mrs Macintyre?"

"She wasn't in, so we decided to try the local churches. There was nothing in the Church Of Scotland records, nor at the Catholic Church. I said to Mrs Gilbert, why don't we try the Wee Free kirk. We went there and sure enough we discovered that the Shields were members there and that Bella had died in the Royal Mental Hospital in Montrose when she was just 32. Oh, they are such a tragic family, Craig."

"Yes, Mum." She was rolling along quite nicely and I didn't want to interrupt her flow too much.

"Anyway, then we went back to see Mrs Macintyre and this time she was home. She said that the Shields were very strict, observed the Sabbath, no drink, you know the kind of people I mean. The lad, James, was killed in a logging accident. He was helping a friend to cut down a tree when it fell the wrong way and crushed him to death. Bella was only twelve when it happened and it seems she went off the rails due to the grief of her brother's death. Mr Shields would beat her and lock her up to make her behave but it didn't make any difference.

Mrs Macintyre said that there was a scandal when Bella was fifteen. There were rumours that Bella was pregnant and she disappeared for a while. The Shields had told everyone who asked that their daughter was living with relatives in Skye but Mrs Macintyre said her mother was convinced that Bella was being held prisoner in the house. No one in Arbroath saw her for over a year and when she reappeared she was a different person. She was very quiet, hardly spoke to anyone, went to Church and that was it."

"What about the baby?"

"Give me a minute, I'm getting to that. Mrs Macintyre said that in 1961, Bella took a strange turn. Some fishermen found her out on the harbour wall, in the middle of a storm. She was lying face up as the waves crashed over her. She had apparently told the group who found her that she wanted to die. They took her to the hospital where she went into a catatonic state. She was committed to the mental hospital up in Montrose soon after. She died there in 1962 without ever coming home. Mrs Macintyre's convinced that the baby was hers and that the Shields hushed it up. Mr Shields was so ashamed that maybe he killed the baby, isn't that terrible?"

"Mum that's just gossip, the baby could have died at birth if there was no medical help. Was there any record of a birth at the house or the church?"

"Not at the kirk but we'll check the registrar's tomorrow. What do you think?"

"You've certainly been busy and it does sound interesting."

"Interesting? It's shocking how young women were treated back then. It's terrible that she ended up in an asylum, you know how bad those places were back then." She was off, she railed for about ten minutes on the injustices of the world in the mid-twentieth century. I had to agree with her, but I wondered if women were treated any better now. My own experience of the past few days certainly made me doubt it.

*

When she had calmed down, we sat down to the cottage pie. During the meal I told her about my own frustrating day at the uni.

When I got on to the subject of Doctor Barclay, she was once again ready to take on the world.

"Someone should tell his wife." She had pulled herself up to her full height, filled with affronted fury.

"No Mum, that's not going to happen. That's for them to sort out."

"But you could send her a letter anonymously, he'd never know."

"Mum, no. It's none of my business. Anyway, she probably has some idea. These guys think they're so clever but half the students at the university had noticed that something was going on between him and Stefania. His wife will know what he's like. Some women just accept their husband's cheating, they see it as a necessary evil that needs to be tolerated. I don't understand it but that doesn't mean I can charge in there and destroy her life. At least if no one tells her, she can pretend that it's not happening."

She shook her head, I wasn't sure if it was at me, the Doctor or his wife.

"Fancy a pudding? I've got a rhubarb pie from the Co. I'll make some nice fresh custard, how does that sound?"

156

She knew that my resistance to her custard was virtually nil, so I agreed eagerly. Twenty minutes later I was content but knew that I needed to solve this case soon or I would be twenty pounds heavier.

When dinner was over and the dishes were washed, I left Mum to her own devices while I went to the spare room with a coffee. I booted up the computer and logged in to Facebook to check the photographs that Alison took at the party.

She had sent me a link to the online album. There were over eighty pictures for me to inspect. It was the kind of collection you would expect from these events. There were candid shots of people drinking, others hamming it up for the camera, pictures of Alison holding the camera at arm's length while hugging a friend and then the aftermath as people passed out from too much partying. There was no sign of the rooftop excursion, she must have missed that highlight.

The young faces that smiled out from the pictures were immortal Gods of their own little worlds. The worst of the struggles of life were yet to touch most of them, that was thankfully still somewhere in their future. At that moment they were partying hard, living life to the full and that was all that mattered.

In one shot, the birthday boy was being held tightly by Hero, as if preventing Gerard from escaping out of the range of the camera's lens. The poor lad looked both scared and miserable. I had the impression that although Hero had teased Gerard a little, there was still a respect and concern for his flatmate. He wanted to help Gerard overcome his shyness but it didn't seem to be having much effect, Gerard's reserve looked entrenched. Whether that was nature or nurture was impossible to say.

The first time through, I skimmed the pictures. On the second pass, I spent a little longer on each one, taking more care to absorb the details. Alicja's joyful face appeared in a couple of shots. In the first, she was in the background as a couple of lads stuck up two fingers at Alison and the camera. In the second, she was part of a featured group of four partygoers. She was wearing a summer dress in pastel blue with white buttons down the front, her hair lifted from her face, styled to heighten her attractive features. She had applied her make-up subtly; with a face as attractive as hers there was no need for anything more. She looked stunning and as I gazed into her soft green eyes, I hoped that I would be able to see her in person, unharmed.

I continued to flick through the album, but there was one picture that I kept returning to. The main subjects were Shelley and Marion but on the right edge of the frame was the face of a dark-haired girl. The left side of her face was nearest to the camera, I couldn't see her eyes properly or the full shape of her head but there was something about her that was familiar.

After another run through of the photographs, I

returned one last time to that same shot as it nibbled at the edges of my memory. I stared at the unknown face for nearly twenty minutes before it hit me. On the line of her jaw, close to the point of her chin, was a tiny mole. It was something that you would never notice with a casual glance. It was in exactly the same place as on the woman in the mortuary. The revelation was horrifying - here was the mystery girl. Or was it? Could I be imagining that I had seen the mole before? I had to contact Danielus.

The phone rang three times before he answered, "Craig?"

"Danielus, hi. Have you got access to a computer with an internet connection?"

"Yes, I have a small laptop with mobile broadband, why?" Once again there was a hope in his voice that I would shatter as quickly as I had inspired it.

"I've found a photograph that I need you to look at. I think I may have found the girl from the mortuary."

"What? Where?"

"She's in a set of photos that were taken on the night of the party."

"Oh no." There were possibilities that spun away from this discovery that were immediately apparent to him.

"I need your e-mail address and I'll send you the link to the album on Facebook. It's picture twenty five."

He gave me the details I had requested and I fired off the mail.

I paced around the room for ten minutes before he rang me back.

"Do you see her?"

"No, I don't understand. These two girls look nothing like the dead woman."

"Not the middle two, the girl who looks as if she is just walking into the frame on the right." I must have sounded exasperated because I certainly felt it.

There was an extended pause before he said, "The hair looks about right but I am not sure."

"Look closely at her jaw line, close to her chin."

Another moment of hesitancy and then I heard an intake of breath. "The little mark, it is the same."

Relieved, I almost cheered. "Yes, that's what I thought."

"Oh dear, if this girl was at the party, does it mean that Alicja is dead also?"

"At the moment it is a coincidence, nothing more." I tried to reassure him but the same thoughts had entered my head.

I didn't point out that there could be another sinister interpretation of my find, that Alicja could have killed the girl and disappeared to avoid being tracked by the police. It seemed unlikely but people do unlikely things when they're drunk or enraged by passion or jealousy. A dead body turns up and at the same time someone goes missing, it could lead the police to certain conclusions that would bring Alicja into focus as a potential killer.

"Do I have to go to the police again?" he asked anxiously.

"No. I'll go and see them. I can show them the picture. We'll take it from there."

"OK. Let me know what happens. Will you have to stop looking for Alicja, now that the police are involved?"

"I'll talk to them and ask them if I can keep searching but they might tell me to back off."

His disappointment coloured his reply. "I understand. Goodbye."

He hung up and left me to consider what was going to happen next.

I realised that the police would be keen to move me aside as they investigated the young woman's death but as always, there was a need for me to see this job through to its conclusion. I wanted to know what had happened to Alicja or alternatively what she had done, it was as simple as that.

Before I could contact the police, I needed to know if anyone at the party knew who the girl was. I hadn't taken Alison's phone number, so I sent her a mail in the hope that she would be online and willing to call me.

In the interim, I called Hero.

"Hero, hi, it's me again. I think the girl who was found on the beach was at the party. I think she's in one of the photographs that Alison took at the party. Could you have a look to see if you know her or remember who she was with?"

'Wow, really? Give me a minute, I'll get my laptop."

I could hear him walking through the house, obviously going for the computer. There was a short hiatus while he organised himself at a desk.

"Alison's a friend on my Facebook anyway. Here it is. I've found the album, what picture is it?"

"Twenty five."

"Right, got it."

"The girl on the right, walking into the picture." I urged him, hoping he would recognise her.

"I'm not sure. She's not a student I recognise but it's a big university."

"Do you think she could be an escort girl, one of Michaels' girls maybe?"

"It's possible but I couldn't say for sure, sorry."

"Do you remember seeing her with Alicja, could she have been the girl Shelley spoke of?"

"Maybe. Sorry, I'm not much help am I?" he asked regretfully.

"It's fine, I can speak to Shelley. Thanks. I've mailed Alison, you don't have her phone number do you?"

"I do. I'll send it to you."

"Cheers, thanks Hero."

I had barely put the phone on the table when it acknowledged the arrival of the text with Alison's number.

Keen to learn more, I rang it immediately.

"Hello?" Alison's voice was quizzical as she obviously didn't recognise my number.

"Alison, hi, it's Craig Campbell, we met earlier."

"Yes."

"It's about one of your photos. In number twenty five there's a woman at the edge of the picture. I think she might be the woman whose body washed up on the beach."

"God, you're, like, kidding aren't you?" There was a degree of panic mingled with excitement in her response.

"I'm afraid not. I was wondering if you could have a look at the picture, see if you remember anything about her." I pushed gently.

"I'll look it up, I've got my laptop here."

I found myself waiting once again for someone at the other end of a phone.

"Yes, I see her. I'm sure she was, like, Eastern European. I remember her, like, talking to the girl you're looking for, they were speaking English but it was difficult to make out, as they had, like, these crazy strong accents. I'm afraid it's a bit, like, hazy as I had quite a bit to drink." Guilt tinged with remorse.

"Is it the same girl that Shelley mentioned?"

"I would imagine so, yeah."

"I don't suppose you caught her name?" I asked, hoping that for once the answer would help me progress.

"No, not her name but I'm sure she came to the party with a student."

"Male or female?"

"Male. Terry Wilson, his name is. I remember it because she was, like, very good looking for Terry. You don't see him with women much, certainly not, like, good-looking girls, anyway. He's a bit strange."

"Do you have his number? I need to speak to him urgently."

"Hero will have it, he's in one or two of Hero's classes. It's through Hero that I know him."

"That's good, thanks for your help, Alison. I'll need to pass this on to the police now, so they'll probably be in touch."

"Right, yes, of course, whatever. Will they, like, interview me?" The thought was obviously one that intrigued her.

"They might, I'm sure they'll be looking to speak to everyone who attended the party if they can. Different people might remember different things that will help them identify the poor girl. They can only make progress on finding who killed her when they know who she is."

"I understand, yes."

"Thanks again for your help, bye for now."

She hung up and I wondered how she would cope

with the next few days, how any of those at the party would deal with being caught up in a murder inquiry. With one dead girl and another missing from the same party, there were bound to be some lives put under close scrutiny. A police investigation can upset the balance of people's lives as they're put under the microscope: the minutiae can be made important, their privacy can be ripped from them.

I dialled the number I had for Fife constabulary. I explained why I was calling and they passed me through to a male officer in the investigating team.

"Incident room, Detective Sergeant Young speaking."

"Hello, my name is Craig Campbell, I have some information regarding the body that was found on Tentsmuir beach."

"OK, sir. Can I take your details?"

"I'll probably be in your records somewhere. I called on Saturday. I'm a private detective, I'm looking for a girl who's been missing for over a week. My client and I went to see the body on Saturday but it wasn't the girl I'm looking for."

"Oh, yes. DC Gray mentioned you. Let me see if I can find your details." His contempt was obvious in every syllable. I could hear him typing slowly on a computer keyboard.

"You're not one of these nuts that likes to waste police time are you?" he asked.

I was tired and irritable, his attitude only served

to make it worse.

"No, officer. I've managed to do what you and your colleagues have failed to do, I have a link to the girl and I know that she was at the same party as the girl who went missing. I was about to tell you some more but if I'm wasting your time, please forgive me."

"Hey, there's no need to be sarcastic." Once again I had opened my mouth and ruffled the feathers of a police officer. It's a habit I really have to break.

"I've got you. Now what do you have for us?"

"One of the students that attended the party has published the photographs on Facebook. The young woman I believe washed up on the beach is probably Eastern European and she may have worked for an escort service that is run out of Dundee by a guy called Michaels. The man who hired her that night is called Terry Wilson, a student at St Andrews University."

"What makes you think it's the same woman?" his voice was conciliatory and I adjusted my tone to match.

"A mole on her left jawline, near her chin. I remembered the mole from our visit to the mortuary and my client also thinks it's the same girl. It may be a coincidence but I don't think so."

"When was this party?"

"A week past on Saturday."

"And it was in St Andrews?"

"Yes in a house in Castle Street."

"Do you think the other girl could be involved?" It was a question I didn't know how to answer but I tried to be truthful.

"I have to be honest and say that it's a possibility. The girls are both Eastern European, one of the witnesses remembers them talking at the party. I haven't found any other connection as yet but who knows."

He absorbed the information I had given him before he asked, "Is there anything else you can tell us?"

"I'll get you a phone number for Wilson and send it over."

"That's a help, thanks. Anything else?"

No, I don't think so. Can you give me an e-mail address and I'll send you the link and the phone number when I get it?"

He supplied the details before asking me to give a statement at the incident office that had been set up in Leuchars. I said I would pop in the following day and then I rang off.

I dialled Hero's number again.

"Hi, Craig."

"I spoke to Alison, she thinks that the girl arrived with Terry Wilson and that you might have his number."

"Aye, I've got it here. You want it?"

"Yes please."

"Will do. Do you think Terry's involved?" he

asked with concern.

"No idea. Do you think he would be capable of murdering someone?"

"He's very quiet, wouldn't seem the type but then you always see these people on telly saying that their neighbour was a quiet person and he turns out to be a serial killer." His imagination was running ahead of him.

"There's no point in speculating at the moment. The police'll ask him some tough questions, I don't doubt. Thanks for your help, I'll try not to bother you again."

"No worries, Craig."

The contact details arrived, including Wilson's address. I copied and pasted it into the mail app on my phone and sent it to the address that DS Young had given me.

*

As the cop hadn't said that I should back off, I decided to keep going. Looking for answers and earning my keep.

I decided that I could maybe get to Wilson first, to see if he knew anything about Alicja.

I dialled the number and waited impatiently as it rang.

"Hi, this is Terry Wilson. Leave a message peeps. It's simples." The last two words were spoken with a fake Russian accent in the style of a popular advert featuring meerkats.

I terminated the call and said, "Shit." I could not move this case forward, no matter what I tried to do. Blocked at every turn, I was getting desperate.

It was nine o'clock but I didn't think that it would be too late to call an escort service. If I could get behind the facade of the Starlight Club I might start to find out what was really going on.

The number that Haines had sent me rang three times before a broad Dundonian accent said, "Starlight Companions, Chantelle speakin', how cin we help ye this evenin'?"

I almost laughed, companions?

"Hi Chantelle, I'm in town tonight and a friend of mine gave me your number. I believe you can offer a gentleman some company for an evening?"

"That's right."

"How much would that cost?"

"It'll depend how much company ye want, ken?"

"Well I was thinking maybe a couple of hours."

"That'll be a hundred quid an hour, if ye want a blow job that's extra, ken? There's nothing kinky, so if yir lookin' tae wear a nappy or ony o' that slappin' yir arse, ye cin forget aboot it and go somewher' else, ken?"

Never having called a service like this before, I wasn't sure what to expect but Chantelle's candid replies were definitely not part of it.

"Err... No, standard companionship is fine. I was wondering if you had something a bit exotic, maybe a

169

foreign companion."

"Scandinanvian, Russkie or Welsh?"

Welsh?!

I began to think it was like ordering a pizza, I wondered if she would offer a drink and some fries with it or maybe ask me if I wanted to go large.

"When you say Russkie?"

"Ye ken, Polish, Latvian an' that. Eastern European types."

"Yes, that's what I'm looking for."

"When dae ye want her?"

"Say about ten. I'll meet her at Discovery Point, my hotel's not far away from there."

"Fine. Cash only tae be paid before ye start, nae cheques. Yir companion'll be Olga the night." I imagined that Olga wouldn't be her real name but it probably fitted the James Bond fantasy of her normal clientele, I was happy to go with it.

"That's great, thank you, Chantelle."

"Yir welcome. Enjoy yir shag." She hung up.

I shook my head. The police shouldn't have too many problems sweeping away Bennett's tawdry little enterprise with employees like Chantelle helping them out.

I called Carol and filled her in with the latest developments.

"Are you sure about this meeting, Craig?"

"I've got to know whether any of the girls know

about Alicja. If she was a part of this service she may have run into danger. I think the other girl, the girl who was killed, was probably involved."

"The police can take it from here, you know. You don't need to do any more."

"I know, darling, but you know that when I've started something I like to see it finished."

"It seems I've got to say this to you all the time, but be careful."

"Yes, ma'am. I'll be home soon, I promise."

"OK. Love you and no trying the merchandise while you're interviewing her." She laughed with little enthusiasm.

"As if."

"Love you."

"Love you, too. Good night."

"Good night."

*

When the bike was parked, I walked to one of Dundee's key tourist attractions, Discovery Point. The RRS Discovery sits in dry dock outside the museum that bears its name. A wooden ship that was built in Dundee, it carried Captain Scott and his crew on journeys of exploration around Antarctica. The museum is popular with families and it gives an insight into the life of the polar explorers in the early years of the 20th Century.

The tourists had long since departed, leaving the ship a strangely eerie sight. The masts were silhouetted against the sky like a giant skeleton. The breeze stirred gently, disturbing the ropes and cables on the venerable ship's deck, making them groan and squeak, the ghosts of winter storms long past.

The rain had finally stopped, the stars twinkled intermittently in the spring twilight as small clouds traversed the sky.

I was about ten minutes early for my appointment. I stood under a street light to ensure that my "companion" would see me.

After a short time a long-legged woman approached me. "Meester Campbell?"

Her accent sounded false, as if she was playing the fantasy role to its extreme.

"Olga?"

"Yes. Are you ready to go to hotel?"

"No, that's not why I'm here."

She backed up slightly and I got a chance to get a better look at her. She was around twenty five, with a pretty face spoiled by make-up applied an inch thick and false eyelashes that looked ridiculous. She wore a light raincoat, opened to reveal a glittering sequinned halter top. A short skirt showed her shapely legs to their full advantage, and they were further emphasised by the four-inch heels she wore on her feet. A substantial purple handbag was draped over her shoulder. The effect was cheap but probably what her regular punters would expect.

"I don't do any kinky. No outside."

"No, I just want to talk. I'll pay you for your time."

"Talk, are you weirdo?" She backed further away.

I held up both hands in a placating gesture, "No. I'm a private detective. I only want to ask you some questions."

"Detective? What questions? I can't talk to police." She was very cautious.

"I'm not that kind of detective. I need to ask you some questions about your work and the girls you work with. I'm looking for a girl who has gone missing, I'm hoping you'll be able to help me."

"I don't know, my boss he will be mad if he knows I speak to detective." Her fear of Michaels and his unpredictable temper was obvious in her concerned expression.

"Honest, I'm not a police detective, I'm only interested in finding out what happened to the girl, that's all. Anyway, how's he going to know? As far as he's concerned you're working tonight."

She hesitated before nodding. "You pay me for two hours you booked, OK?"

"OK, no problem." I wondered how that would look on my expense statement, I'm not sure the taxman would be impressed.

"You want to talk here?"

"No, I thought we could go along to the bar, the one next to the hotel, just along the road a bit."

"OK."

As we walked I started to ask her some questions.

"Is Olga your real name?"

"No, it is Ruta. They make me change it, say Olga is good name for escort."

"Where do you come from, Ruta?"

"Kraków, Poland."

"How long have you been in Scotland?"

"Two years."

She was an unwilling subject for my interview but I hoped that she would maybe relax when we were settled in the pub.

When we arrived at the bar, she found a seat while I ordered a vodka with lemonade for her and a coke for me. We had obviously caused a stir, it might have been my imagination but there seemed to be plenty of tongues wagging: Ruta's mode of dress was less than subtle and it was easy to imagine what the topic of conversation was among our fellow patrons. Thankfully it was too late for any families to be in for a meal.

The bar was about half full, some diners finishing their meals, others sipping wine, huddled in romantic conversations. It was typical of the fake cosiness of that style of restaurant. Average food packaged with olde worlde charm in the hope the customers wouldn't notice.

Olga had chosen a table close to the window, softly lit by a dimmed overhead spotlight and a flickering candle in a lamp.

"How did you end up with Michaels?" I asked

when we were comfortable.

"I worked in farm near Carnoustie. It was hard work, we work long time and it is sore on back and hands. A man there say that he will take me to meet a man who will pay me more for less work. It was Mr Michaels, he said I could get more money for dancing." The fake accent had been dropped when she dropped the fake name; her own accent was less like a Bond villain parody.

"Only dancing?"

"Yes, at first. Then he say I can earn much more if I make sex with men. I was not sure but I spoke with one of girls who said that he paid much more money and he look after girls."

"And does he?"

"He pay us and gives us nice flat to live although we have to share with other girls. He protects us. He beats any man who does not pay or is rough with us."

She paused to sip her drink, as if considering what she was about to say. "I do it for money but some of the girls like the sex thing. You get more money for less work than the farm, I just switch off and think of the money. I don't have to work every night. But you must not tell anyone I tell you this."

"That's OK, I'll keep this between us. Now, the girl I'm looking for is also Polish, Alicja Symanski."

"I do not know this name."

"I've got a photograph, if you would take a look."

I showed her Stefania and Alicja's picture on my

phone.

"No, I have not seen these girls." She shook her head vigorously as if to reassure me of her honesty.

"OK. I've got another one I would like you to look at."

This time I showed her the picture from the Facebook album of the party.

She studied it for a short time before she said, " I do not know these but this one, I remember."

She had pointed to the main girls in the picture before she picked out the murdered girl.

"How do you know her?"

"She worked at club. We all have to take turn dancing and doing the sex." I was pleased that my instinct had been right.

"Do you know her name?"

"She was called Christina but I don't know if that is her real name."

"That's great, Ruta, this is a huge help. Do you remember when you last spoke to her?"

"It was three weeks since we worked in club together. I have not seen her since then."

"Do you know anything about her?"

"Why do you ask these questions about this woman, if she is not the one you look for?"

"Because I think she may be the woman who was found dead on a beach not far from here."

My words were like a slap in the face. The shock

altered her features as she stared at the photograph again.

"I can't believe such a thing could happen." She was close to tears.

"I have to go to the police tomorrow, if there is even the slightest little detail you could add, it might help to identify her properly and to let her family know what has happened."

"I did not talk much to her but I know that she was not from Poland. I had to speak English with her. I think she came from Latvia or Lithuania. I can't remember which one."

"Do you know where she lived in Dundee?"

"No, but it will be with other girls from the club. He insist we live where he can get hold of us. He has flats across city, two or three girls live in each."

"Michaels?"

"Yes."

"Has ever been violent with any of the girls?"

"He is OK as long as you do as he tells you. He pays us what we earn. He is not so nice if you don't do as he says. I have seen him slap girls."

"Why don't you leave? Find other work."

"I make money to send home to my family. The money is better than the work I have before, it is not easy to make that money other ways. I do not tell my family what I do, they think I still work on farm."

"Would he hurt you if you leave?"

She considered it and then replied, "I think, maybe. I do not know for sure."

"Do you know where Michaels was a week past Saturday?"

She thought for a moment before she said, "At club I think. I wasn't there, I had to do this."

"Could you ask the other girls if he was there, please?"

"Yes. I will ask girls at flat. Karina was at club that night, I think."

"Thanks, that would be a help. What about your clients, have there been any that have hurt you or any of the other girls?"

"Many of the girls have had this happen. Men think they can do anything to you when they pay for you. Some are drunk and can't get their thing to work. They blame girl and hit them. Others just like to hit, thinks it makes them big man." There were further hints of tears.

"What does Michaels say about that?"

"One girl was beaten by the man she was with, he broke her bone here." She pointed to her cheek. "Michaels found man and he got some men to break both his legs. He doesn't like it if other men hurt girls."

I was pretty sure that he would be protecting his financial assets rather than any human concern for the girls.

"Do you know how many girls work for Michaels?"

"There are many, between club and companions. Some work here in Dundee, others in Perth and Fife."

"Thanks Ruta, you've been a big help. I'm going to speak to Michaels, I won't tell him we've spoken, I promise."

"Please, you must not tell him anything."

"I won't, I need to tell him about Christina. I need to see if he was involved in her death and if there's a possible connection to Alicja."

"OK."

"I think you should think about going home and getting a proper job, you're too good for this kind of life. Any woman is too good for this work, you understand."

"I do, but it is not easy to walk away like you say. I will think about it."

I reached into the inside pocket of my jacket and retrieved the journal I had found in the caravan. "Can you do me a favour? This is Alicja's diary. There might be something that can tell me what she was thinking in the days before she disappeared. Unfortunately, my Polish is non-existent."

She understood what I was asking. "I will read it and tell you."

"Thanks, I really appreciate this. Here's my card, give me a ring if you hear anything about what Michaels was up to that Saturday night."

"OK."

We finished our drinks and stepped out into the

pleasant spring night. I handed her the money as discreetly as possible, she thanked me and walked off into the dark. I watched her go with a heavy heart. Prostitution was an age-old profession but the women were always the ones to suffer. It would be Ruta that would be prosecuted if she was ever caught, the man who hired her would probably get a slapped wrist. I didn't have any answers, but I wished there was a better way. Everywhere I looked in this case there were women being treated abysmally by men. It seems that equality is a distant dream, even now.

The Starlight club was within walking distance, and it was time to get Michaels talking. I checked my watch. It was half past ten. The club wouldn't close for a couple of hours yet so I had to decide whether to try to get in or to wait until Michaels appeared when business was over for the night.

In the end I decided I didn't fancy creating a scene in the club, which was inevitable after I had provoked him and his hired goon on my last visit. I didn't think my ribs could take a second round with McLaghan.

There was a burger place along from the hotel that served slops until late. I went in and drank awful coffee until they threw me out at midnight.

*

The air was now warm and still, the sky sparkling with distant jewels. I walked in the general direction of the club and as I passed on the opposite side of the street, I could see the customers filing out after their night of leering at the dancers, some staggering, some slithering.

The girls were next to appear. There were five of them, they all hugged before splitting into two groups and headed off in separate directions.

I ran to where I had parked the bike as I had to be ready for Michaels when he came out. My plan was simple, I would follow him back to his house and challenge him there. I hoped that he wouldn't have any resident thugs, I somehow didn't think he would be quite as much of a hard man if there was no muscle around to protect him.

I rode the bike up to where I could see the club's entrance. I sat for half an hour before Michaels emerged with McLaghan and an older woman. There was a brief conversation before they dispersed.

I kept my eye on Michaels as he crossed to a car park on the opposite side of Union Street. There were only four or five cars parked. The lights on an Audi A4 blinked as he disabled the alarm and unlocked the doors. I waited until I had some sense of the direction he was going to go. I picked him up as he headed east. Expecting him to live in Dundee, I was surprised when he indicated towards the ramp for the Tay Bridge. I kept a distance of about 100 yards between the bike and the car. I tailed him as he turned left after crossing the bridge and down to Tay Street. At the junction he turned right, heading for Tayport, which was a mile or so round the headland. The road was extremely quiet and I hung back about 200 yards, hoping to avoid being seen. A short time later he entered Tayport village and I accelerated a little as I didn't want to lose him in the maze of little streets. I followed him to a small estate of modern houses at the eastern end of the village. The little cul-de-sac was the picture of suburban order, neat little boxes, trimmed lawns and sales rep family saloons.

I parked at the end of the little street and waited for a few minutes to allow him to settle before I approached the white door. The house was a pretty standard suburban detached. Two or three bedrooms, it was set in a landscaped garden with an attached garage. I wondered if Michaels' neighbours knew how he earned a living. Somehow I doubted it.

A security light illuminated my approach as I rang the bell. There was a long pause. I peered through the door's glass panels and could see that someone was responding. The door had three locks and they tumbled one after the other before it finally opened and there was Michaels, standing with a very large cleaver, poised to react to any attack.

"Oh fuck, what d'you want?" Fear and relief wrestled for dominance on his features.

"Hey, I think you better put that away."

"Fuck off, I've got fuck all to say t'ye."

"I want to talk, I think you need to hear what I've got to say."

"Fuck off." He motioned to close the door but

years of insurance investigations had taught me how to get my foot in the door.

"Look, we can do this here, maybe I'll talk loud enough to attract your neighbours' attention, or we can go in and conduct our business in private." I wasn't sure where the bravado was coming from. Ever since Davie Stone had tried to carve me like a Christmas turkey, I was extremely nervous around knives and a cleaver was a very large knife.

"Get in." He created enough space for me to walk through into a beige wallpapered hall. He gestured with the cleaver to a door on the right of the hall.

I walked into a spartan living room. The same beige wallpaper covered the walls, the same sand-coloured carpet covered the floor. There was a sofa and a chair, a standing lamp, a television with a Blu-ray player and a modern gas fire set into the wall. There were no pictures or ornaments. It looked like a show house: I certainly couldn't criticise his housekeeping.

He walked in behind me, still bearing the cleaver.

"I think you can put that away. What are you so nervous about, anyway?"

"Ye've got to look after yirself these days. Ye don't know what kind of scum can tern up at yir door," he said pointedly before he walked out again and returned minus the weapon.

"What the fuck you doing? Coming to me house, as if the club wasn't bad enough."

I handed him the photograph that included

Christina.

"I believe you know the woman on the right."

He studied it, peering like someone who was too vain to admit he needed glasses.

"Maybe."

"Look, I need you to stop pissing around because if the police come calling they won't be as patient as I'm being. I believe this girl was working for you. I know that she was at the same party as the girl I'm looking for. I know that she's lying on a mortuary slab and I'm wondering if you put her there."

"What? I don't know nuttin' about dat. I thought she'd just taken off back to wherever de fuck she came from." His reaction seemed genuine but it was hard to tell with someone who was a compulsive, long-time liar.

"Tell me what you do know because I'm getting kinda anxious to find out what happened that night."

"She was with one of dem students, one of the sad little pricks who can't get any for demselves. She was supposed to just be with 'im at the party, that was it."

"Is he a regular?"

"I don't know, it's not like I keep a fuckin' data-base." His reply dripped with sarcasm.

"Have you had problems with any of the students before?"

"There's been the occasional one who decided he don't want to pay. I normally sort dat out wit' no problem."

"I can imagine. Where were you that Saturday night?"

"At the club, where I am every fuckin' night."

"You weren't in St Andrews?"

"What de fuck would I be doing dere?"

"I don't know. How do the girls get home? I know you like to keep them stabled in Dundee."

"McLaghan picks them up or they get a taxi."

"Did he pick them up on that Saturday?"

"I think so, yeah. Taxis are too fuckin' expensive."

"If you know who this girl is you can't ignore it. You need to let the police know."

"Me talk to de rozzers? You are a fuckin' comedian, you should be on Live At The Apollo. I can't do dat, people like me don't talk to any pigs, in case someone gets the wrong idea and before you know it, someone turns me into bacon."

"That's up to you but you can bet they are going to be all over you for this. You've got a reputation for violence against women, they already know about your business interests. You don't go to them and you're in for a hard time of it. How are those people you mentioned going to feel if their business goes down the tubes in Dundee? From what I hear you've not really covered yourself in glory in Liverpool or Glasgow. Three fuck-ups might just be one too many."

"Dere ye go shootin' yir gob off again about summin' you know nuttin' about. I don't care what a gobshite like you says, it's not werth me going to the cops."

"Fine. I'm going to see them tomorrow. I have to tell them what I know. They need to find out the girl's real name, then they can begin the investigation and let her family know. Have a think about doing the right thing, for once in your shitty little life."

I stood and walked out before he could reply.

TUESDAY 20TH APRIL, 2010

The next day I was back on the road to St Andrews and in particular the Rose Farm. I was beginning to feel like a commuter.

Michaels' attitude hadn't surprised me; he had little respect for himself, never mind other people. He couldn't care less about the girls that worked in his slimy little empire, they were just products to be sold.

The one man I wanted to talk to more than any other was Bennett. The obnoxious little cretin was like a burr in my leathers, a constant irritant.

I rode the bike harder than I normally would to try to release some of the frustration I felt at the constant diversions and road blocks I had encountered in the case.

I arrived at the farm around ten o'clock and parked the Ducati in the main farmyard. I was about to knock on the farmhouse door when I heard a shout.

"Mr Campbell."

I turned to see Colin Rose making his way up from the workers' caravans. He looked like he had been hiking, he had a bag over his shoulder and a pair of stout walking boots on his feet.

"Mr Rose."

"Please, Mr Rose is in the house, I'm Colin."

"OK, Colin it is then." He seemed to have warmed to me since our last encounter, or maybe this was his identical twin.

"Are you here to see Danielus, is there news?"

"No, I'm here to speak to Neil." I was expecting a verbal blast in reply but I was pleasantly surprised.

"He's out supervising the troops, there's some cabbage being harvested."

"Do you think I can speak to him?"

He nodded. "That's fine as long as you don't distract him too much."

"How do I find him?"

"Head back out the main path, turn right. Go about a mile and you'll see a track on the left. They're in the second field on the right up that track." He was affable and helpful, I didn't know what had changed in the three days since we had last met but at least it was a change for the better.

I said thanks, climbed back on board the bike and was turning into the track within five minutes. The rough road surface played havoc with the suspension and my teeth were rattled by the time I brought the bike to a halt next to a hawthorn hedge.

There was a group of around twelve people working across the furrows of the field. The smell of cabbage would have sent a vegetarian into rapture but it only reminded me of Boxing Day when I was a kid and the unfortunate atmosphere that the previous day's dinner had generated.

I could see a blue Land Rover parked in one corner. Bennett was sitting in it reading a newspaper, smoking a cigarette, his feet like rabbit's ears as they rested on the dashboard. The window was open and he blew the smoke out of it like a guilty teenager puffing in his bedroom. The smell of something other than tobacco drifted over to me.

I made my way along the fence to the car. He obviously noticed my approach but chose to ignore me, continuing to smoke and read. I knocked on the passenger side window. He looked up as if surprised and promptly went back to browsing his paper.

Stressed, frustrated and angry, I walked around the vehicle, opened his door and dragged him out by his arm before he could react. The newspaper pages separated and caught on the breeze, which scattered them across the brown earth like the seeds of an enormous tree. His strange-smelling cigarette fell into a puddle in a furrow.

"What the fuck?" he exclaimed.

I picked him up, grabbed him by the throat and pinned him against the blue bonnet of the ageing car.

"Look, your wee hard man routine might work with those poor sods but not with me." I indicated the farm workers.

"I'm going to ask you a few questions and you better be in a mood to talk because believe me, I have had enough of everybody lying to me. A girl's life might be at stake. Do you understand?"

"Whit's your problem? You're a psycho. Fuck sake, man."

I added further intimidation to my voice. "I said, do you understand?"

"Aye, aye."

I eased my grip on him a little as I noticed the work seemed to have ground to a halt in the field. I didn't want to create too much of a spectacle.

"Are you willing to answer my questions without your usual bullshit?"

"Aye, fuck aye. Whit's yir problem? Ye're a fuckin' nutter, do you know that?"

I removed my hands from him and allowed him to compose himself. He rubbed his neck where my hand had been. Now that I could see him close up my impression didn't improve from my first encounter. There was a lot about him that repulsed me apart from his winning personality. His skin was filthy, blackheads punctuating it like a mediaeval disease, his face had an unhealthy tinge of mustard yellow as if he had liver problems: his clothes were engrained with enough dirt to grow a crop in and there was a faint but distinct smell of alcohol combined with a hint of cannabis. It was hard to believe that he had ever been disciplined enough to serve as a soldier.

"Look, I don't know anything about that Polack bint, ken. Ah've already tellt ye that." He had regained some of his charm.

"I'd imagine that what you don't know would fill volumes but let me ask some questions and then I'll decide what you know or don't know about this."

He stood with his arms crossed, like a sullen child that had been denied a treat. The work in the field had resumed as our conflict had proved to be less entertaining than they were hoping for. I was pretty sure that there was only one person they would be supporting.

"When was the last time you saw Alicja?"

"The Saturday moarnin' afore she fucked off."

"And how was she?"

"How the fuck should ah know? Ah'm nae psychologist, she could have hud her period or bin up the duff for aw ken."

I resisted an urge to grab him again. "I'm not looking for a clinical diagnosis, I'm asking for your impression."

"Och, she wis awright. Probably happier than usual, ah heard her tell that Stephanie wan that she wis lookin' forward to the perty, ken?"

"Stefania."

"Aye, whitever." He shrugged.

"There was nothing about her that made you think she was ready to leave?"

"Naw but she's a bird. Ye never know wi' them. They can just flip, change like the weather."

"Did you ever have a problem with her?"

He stopped leaning on the car and drew himself up indignantly. "Whit the fuck ye tryin' tae say? That I hud somethin' tae dae wi' her disappearin'? Ah didnae like the stupid cow but ah've got nothin' tae dae wi' her fuckin' aff back tae whitever shite hole she came fae." His reaction was passionate but so much of him was a facade it was hard to gauge what was real and what was his sense of self-preservation.

"I'm trying to work out what might have happened. If she had an argument with you or anyone else it might have been enough to make her leave. Did you have an argument or a fight with her?"

"Naw. Maybe you should be askin' that black, they like a bit white tail. Maybe she wisnae up for it."

I shook my head, clenched my fists before taking a long deep breath and then relaxed my hands.

"Other than your Ku Klux Klan leanings, do you have any reason to suspect George had something to do with this?"

"He's fucked off as well. Probably done her in and is aff runnin' back tae darkie land."

"What are you talking about?"

"He's done a runner. Naebody's seen him since yesterday moarning. Didnae show fur 'is shift.

192

Didnae appear at the caravan last night. He's fired if he dares tae show his black face again."

George disappearing could be a coincidence. He may have been sick of dealing with the scum that was standing in front of me. However, I couldn't dismiss it completely, I felt it might be related, I wasn't sure how. Could George have killed Alicja? If he had why had he stuck around for over a week. It was too much to think about as I stood in that field but it was something I would have to consider.

"Do you have anything constructive to offer? Do you know of anyone with a genuine reason to bear a grudge against Alicja?"

He pretended to think and it was like watching the mechanism of Big Ben turning over.

"Fuck knows."

"What about Robbie Michaels? Is he a pal of yours?"

"Who?" his ugly features arranged into a quizzical look that managed to make him appear comical.

"Michaels. The Scouse pimp working out of Dundee. He told me that he had some help finding girls among the farm workers. I think that you might be his man at Rose Farm."

"Are ye no' takin' yir tablets or somethin'? Ah don't ken anythin' aboot a Michaels." He smirked at me. I couldn't tell if he was lying or not, the bully's ugly grimace had returned. I decided that I probably wasn't going to get the truth from him until I had the facts to back it up; even then he might keep repeating his denials.

I looked at the dishevelled and pathetic figure in front of me and wondered what could make someone go from a decorated serviceman to the disgusting collection of atoms that stood before me.

I decided to take a different approach. "What happened when you were in the army?"

He was discomfited by my change of tack.

"Whit dae ye want tae ken that fur?' He was as defensive as Colin Rose had been. Painful memories, deeply buried, were resurfacing.

"Call it curiosity."

"None o' yir business, right?"

"You were in the Balkans?"

"Aye, Bosnia," he replied reluctantly.

"Tough?"

"You fuckin' bet yir life it wis but whit's it goat tae dae wi' some wee lassie disappearin'?"

"Maybe nothing. Just call it natural inquisitiveness, it's a good trait to have when you're in my job."

"Away stick yir nose somewhere else. Ah've goat nothin tae say tae ye, ken."

"If I find you knew something and you didn't tell me, I'll be back and I won't be so gentle next time." I lowered my voice and edged towards him to emphasise the threat. He backed against the Land Rover again. I smiled and turned away.

"Aye, you're a big man right enough. Maybe you should watch yir back, ye never ken who yir messin' wi."

I ignored his pathetic bluster and continued walking, seething at myself for my lack of control. I began to wonder what was happening to me. Was my new role beginning to change me into someone I didn't recognise or was it the frustration taking over? It was a disturbing thought but not as disturbing as thinking that I wasn't any nearer to finding a girl who was relying on me, even if she didn't know me.

I was about to ride to Leuchars when I decided now might be a good time to talk to some of the other workers on the farm. They might be able to add some detail on Alicja's state of mind or have noticed someone taking an unhealthy interest in her.

I shouted to Bennett, "I'm going to speak to the workers, I'll not keep them long."

He ignored me, which I took as his agreement for me to interview them.

I steered the bike along the edge of the field to where the machines and people went about their business.

I stopped about twenty metres from where the farm staff were bent over, slicing the cabbage from the plants and placing them in polythene bags. The bags were then placed on plastic trays on a mobile rig awaiting a tractor to take them to the next stage of their journey to the supermarket and finally the consumer's table.

The work halted as I took off my helmet. I couldn't see Danielus but Stefania was one of the harvesters.

"Mr Campbell, you have news?"

"I'm afraid not Stefania, I was hoping to ask some questions of your colleagues. They might remember something that will help me."

Stefania turned to her work mates and said something in Polish followed by, "Please come, Mr Campbell wants to ask you about Alicja."

She then turned back to me and said, "There are couple people whose English is not so good. I will try translate for you."

"Thanks."

The twelve workers gathered round like a lynch mob from a Hammer horror movie, each armed with a knife that was between six and eight inches long. I tried to keep the distracting sight out of mind as I began.

"Thank you for giving me your time, I won't keep you long. Can anyone tell me if they have seen someone taking an interest in Alicja, a delivery man or a driver, maybe?"

Stefania translated my question but the assembled workers were universal in the shaking of their heads.

"Do any of you know how Alicja was before she disappeared? Was she worried about something or scared of somebody?"

After the pause for Stefania's translation a Polish

speaking man answered her.

"He say that she did not like him." She gestured with her head towards Bennett at the other end of the field. "He say she was not frightened but she did not want to work with him any more. Like I said in caravan."

"I think she find a new boyfriend." This came from a stocky woman with dark red hair. Her accent was slightly different from Stefania, whether she was from another part of Poland or another country, I couldn't be sure.

"Why do you say that?" I asked her directly.

"She had been happy but not about work. I ask her but she said it was secret. She was going to tell after the party."

"What do you think was going to happen at the party?"

"I not sure but she was looking forward to it very much."

"OK thanks. If you remember anything, no matter how insignificant, please contact me." I handed them each one of my cards, thanked them again and let them get back to their labour. It was another frustrating conversation; little hints were all I could glean from anyone.

I climbed aboard the Ducati and headed for Leuchars.

*

As I entered St Andrews I could feel my phone

vibrating in my pocket. I pulled in to the side of the road close to Janetta's, St Andrews' famous ice cream parlour. My Ducati joined around twenty Harley Davidsons and Honda Goldwings that were also parked there. The bikers were resting against their bikes with their ice cream cones and wafers, the flavoured ice creams decorated in chocolate sprinkles and raspberry sauce. It was an incongruous sight to see the hairy middle-aged men in full black leathers enjoying their treat like they were out on a school trip.

I lifted the phone from my pocket. I didn't recognise the number on the missed call list but I returned the call thinking that it might be the police.

"Hello, Mr Campbell?" A familiar voice.

"Hi, yes it's me."

"It's Ruta, I spoke to Karina. She tells me that Michaels went to St Andrews on the Saturday night. She say that Christina phoned to say that she was going to quit. The man she was with wanted her to do things she did not like. She told Michaels that she was finished. He was very mad. McLaghan was supposed to get Christina from St Andrews but he was in hospital after a fight at the door of club. The boss' assistant, Brenda, say that she will phone taxi but Michaels he said no, he would get her. Karina said that the girls were scared of him, he was shouting and swearing."

"What time did this happen?"

"Before girls left club at end of night."

"Thanks Ruta, and thank Karina for me. I need to tell the police about this. Have you had a chance to check the journal?"

"I am going to read it later, I will call if I find something."

"Thanks again."

I left the Walls' angels to their desserts and raced away towards Leuchars. Now I was convinced that Michaels had killed Christina. What about Alicja? Was he involved in her disappearance and maybe even murder? Maybe she saw him with Christina. I wasn't sure exactly but I needed to find out.

*

My pulse quickened as I considered the possibility of finally making some progress. I began the journey to Leuchars and the incident room the police had set up in the town. I was entering the town's boundaries when a thought suddenly occurred to me. What if I had spooked Michaels last night? I cursed at my own stupidity and the fact that I had spoken to him. If he thought someone was on to him, he might decide to bolt before the police could arrest him. If he was guilty of Christina's murder as I now believed, my visit may have done enough to persuade him that he should get as far away from Dundee as he could.

I passed the portable office that the police had placed in the car park of a disused pub. I decided that I would speak to them after I checked on Michaels.

I could feel an anxious form of excitement build

ing as I returned to the delightful village of Tayport. I found my way back to Michaels' cul-de-sac. I had opted to park at the end of the short road and was glad I did.

From my vantage point I could see Michaels' house. His Audi was parked outside with the boot and back doors open. I watched for a couple of minutes before he appeared with a packing case that he placed in the rear seat before going back into the house.

I realised that my visit had been enough to give him cause for concern. I backed the bike up a little, removed my helmet and reached for my phone. I had stored the incident room number the policeman had given me the previous night.

After two rings it was answered. "Leuchars police incident room, Detective Sergeant Knowles speaking."

"Hi, my name is Craig Campbell, I called last night." I realised I was speaking in a hushed tone, which was pointless as there was no way Michaels could hear me.

"Yes, Mr Campbell, my colleague left me a note to say that you would be coming in."

"That was the plan but I need you to come to me."

"Oh?" He sounded a little annoyed at my presumption.

"It's Robbie Michaels, I think he murdered the girl you found at Tentsmuir and he's packing his car as if he plans to do a runner."

"What makes you think it was him?"

I fired the sentences at him. "I don't know how much you know about the guy, detective, but he has a history of violence against women that work for him. He runs a strip joint in Dundee that acts as a front for his pimping activities. The girl that was murdered worked as a dancer and prostitute for him under the name Christina.

She was sent to a job in St Andrews with some student a week past Saturday. She had a problem with her client and told Michaels that she was finished. He didn't take it too well and went to pick her up. I think he was angry enough to kill her and dump her body."

"Have you got witnesses?"

"Some of the other girls had heard him going nuts about Christina."

"Where are you?"

"I'm at the end of his road." I gave him the street name.

"Right, I'll send my colleague to get a warrant for his car and home. If she was there we'll find it. I'll come to you and we'll keep an eye on him until we get organised." He sounded energised and eager to catch a killer.

"OK. What do you want me to do if he leaves before you get here?"

"Ring me and we'll get a patrol car to pick him

up."

"OK. Please hurry."

*

Twenty minutes later I was sitting in Detective Knowles' Vauxhall Insignia, close to where I'd left my bike. Michaels had added another two boxes to the one he had already put in the car. He had shut the boot and doors before he retreated indoors again.

The clock seemed to move like it was on the event horizon of a black hole, each second longer than the last.

After another hour of our impatient stake out, a call came through from a female officer on DS Knowles' radio.

"DC Welch to DS Knowles."

"Go ahead, DC Welch."

"We've got the warrant, Sarge. Be with you in thirty minutes."

"Understood."

He turned to me. "All we have to do is sit tight until they arrive."

DS Knowles was in his late thirties with dark hair that was beginning to show flecks of grey. Intense blue eyes gazed out of a strong face. He looked physically fit and carried little excess weight. As far removed from the television's stereotypical doughnut and curry loving cop as you could get.

Another ten minutes had past when Michaels came through his front door again. He began turning keys in the extravagant array of locks on the door.

"Shit!" DS Knowles and I exclaimed simultaneously.

"Right, this might get a bit hairy." Knowles turned the key to start the engine.

We watched as Michaels completed his task and got behind the wheel of his car. He reversed out of his drive and as he moved along the road DS Knowles pulled his car to cover the entrance to the cul-de-sac, which boxed Michaels in. I could see Michaels' face as he recognised me, panic registering at the same time as he realised who else was beside me. I thought he was going to ram the side of the Insignia but he hammered on the brakes and opened his door.

Knowles reacted quickly, out of the car and on Michaels' heels before the killer had run five strides. Michaels was running back towards his house, the police officer at his back. Michaels vaulted a small fence as Knowles closed in. They then disappeared out of my sight.

I finally let a breath go that I had held since Michaels had begun to drive towards us.

I opened the car window, not sure what to do while the chase continued. Five minutes of inactivity was finally interrupted by the shouts of Michaels as DS Knowles marched him back, handcuffs restraining the truculent pimp.

I got out of the car. When Michaels saw me, he shouted in my direction. "Is dis your fuckin' fault?"

"No Robbie, I think you'll find its all your own work. What happened, Robbie? Did Christina refuse to succumb to your charms or was it just she had enough of lying on her back making money for you?"

"Fuck you. You're in so much trouble, there are people who will seriously hert you." He tried to break Knowles' grip but the detective's hold was firm.

I was surprisingly calm as I answered, "Maybe. But I think you're the one who might have to worry about pain coming his way. Your cousins aren't going to be happy that your temper made you balls it up again. Maybe you'll have to watch your back in whatever nick they send you to."

"Fuck you, I'll kill you, I'll kill you." His eyes bulged and saliva dripped from his mouth as he raved at me. The burn scar on his neck contrasted with the bright red of his face.

"What happened to Alicja? Was she just a witness you had to get rid of?" I shouted my own rage back at him.

"Fuck off, none o' dis has anythin' to do with me. I never met the skanky slag."

"Shut up, Michaels. Get in the car." DS Knowles forced him into the rear of his car and locked it.

"We'll wait on the others getting here, I'll get someone to take bawheid here to the station in St Andrews, while we do the search."

Michaels sat glaring at me and trying to make threatening gesture despite his restraints.

A fleet of two patrol cars, an unmarked Mondeo and a transit van pulled up ten minutes later. Michaels was dispatched with a detective and a uniformed constable for company.

Knowles moved his car up the cul-de-sac and the rest of the small fleet followed.

A team of three SOCO's appeared from the transit van and began to dress themselves in their attractive white protective suits, face masks and blue covers for their shoes.

Another hour passed as the technicians and police officers moved in and out of Michaels' house. Boxes were loaded into the van from both Michaels' car and his home.

A curious neighbour offered to make tea and coffee. She appeared with a tray of cups and a plate of biscuits, which were quickly consumed by myself, DS Knowles and his DCI, whose name was McArdle.

Hunger and thirst satisfied, I sat back on my bike and waited on the police to finish their business.

When DS Knowles came back towards me, he flashed a big grin at me. "Did you enjoy winding him up? It looks like you were right. There's blood on the seat in the car, hopefully it'll be a match to the girl's."

"Is it enough?"

"I think with motive, opportunity and some physical evidence, it looks good. We'll check the CCTV footage from that night and we'll hopefully catch the two of them in the car together. That would probably seal it."

"Great. It would be good if we could find out her real name and get word to her family."

"Aye, true enough. Maybe some of his little gang at the club will be a little more helpful. I doubt any of them will fancy being linked to a murder."

"What about Alicja? Any sign?"

"Not that we can see. We'll need to test the DNA of the blood we found. It might be the girl you're looking for but we can't be sure until then."

Despite the capture of Michaels, I felt suddenly deflated. I had hoped that something might help me in my search for Alicja but it wasn't to be. I was no further forward than I had been last night.

Tired and depressed I decided to leave them to it.

"You'll let me know if you hear anything won't you?" I asked the Sergeant.

"Will do, Craig. Thanks for your help, you did good today. We'll need a statement from you, if you could pop in some time it would be appreciated."

"Will do. Cheers." I gave him a brief wave as I pulled away from the cul-de-sac.

*

The journey to Arbroath did nothing to lighten my mood. By the time I parked in the street where Mum lives, I felt like giving Danielus his money back.

Mum was bright and cheery when I walked into the living room. "Hello, son. You look a bit down, what's up?"

"Robbie Michaels has been arrested for the murder of Christina, the girl that was found on the beach."

"That's good news, isn't it?" she asked, confused by my lack of exuberance.

"Yes, of course. It's just that the police haven't found anything to connect him to Alicja's disappearance. At least not yet. I'm no further forward in finding her and I don't know what to do."

"Something'll come up. At least that rogue Michaels is where he should be."

"I know." I smiled to let her see that I was glad of her support.

"There's some pasta with tomato sauce if you'd like that for dinner."

"Aye, that's fine."

She went to the kitchen as the door bell rang.

"Get that, would you, son? It might be the paper boy."

I did as she requested and opened the door to a sight that lifted my spirits. Carol threw her bag into the hall, jumped on me and kissed me fiercely.

"Hello, you." Her broad grin was infectious and I grinned back with renewed energy.

"Hello yourself. What are you doing here?"

"I wanted to come and see your mum." Se paused before adding, "Oh and you. I was owed some time from work, so I thought I'd come and keep you company."

"Come here." We embraced in the hall after I shut the door.

My mother arrived to see what all the fuss was about.

"Carol, hello pet. It's good to see you. It might cheer misery guts up a bit." She lifted Carol's bag and put it in the spare room.

"Come away through and we'll get you some dinner."

"That would be great Mrs Campbell."

"I've told you before, Moira or Mum if you like but never Mrs Campbell."

"OK, Mum."

"I'll get the dinner sorted and you two can have a blether."

Carol and I sat in the living room. I told her all the events of the day and like Mum, she tried to get me to focus on the positives.

"You never know, Craig, something could still help you find Alicja. Keep trying for a while longer, unless Danielus wants you to quit."

"You're right, I'll go see him tomorrow and ask him what he wants to do. With everything that's happened, the police are probably going to be taking a closer look at her disappearance anyway."

Over dinner the three of us enjoyed a bottle of Pinot Grigio that Carol had brought with her.

"I hear you're a bit of a sleuth as well, Mum," Carol suggested.

"Oh, did he tell you? It's quite exciting. We were at the registry office today but there was no birth registered for anyone in the house. I think they covered it up, I think that they were so ashamed of what their daughter had done they didn't tell anyone."

"It would have been a scandal back then, particularly in a small community."

I watched as the two of them enjoyed speculating what might have happened. It was good to see them getting on so well, it certainly made my life easier.

"I'm going to phone the mortuary tomorrow and see what they found," Mum said.

"I'll give you a hand with your investigations if you like," said Carol.

Oh crap, I thought, but kept it firmly to myself.

"That would be great, Carol. I can see why he likes doing this detective stuff." Mum beamed a contented smile.

I left them to make their grand plans, while I had a shower to relieve some of the aches that were still niggling at me.

WEDNESDAY 21ST APRIL, 2010

I awoke with Carol nestled against my chest. She was sleeping soundly and I took a moment to study her. Her blonde hair was in disarray on the pillow from sleep, she wore no make up and still she looked like a Hollywood starlet. She had brought so much to my life in a short time and I knew that our relationship was becoming something very special.

I eased my arm from under her head and got dressed. She had said nothing about the rainbow of fading bruises across my thighs and ribs but she had shaken her head in gentle admonition.

I made myself a strong morning coffee, a slice of toast and settled down with the MacBook to check my e-mail.

After clearing the junk and answering another joke-filled mail from Li, I discovered a note from Hero. He had forwarded a link to some videos that had been taken on the night of the party by a girl who had been on the roof. I typed a short reply to thank him before clicking on the URL, with little hope of finding anything.

I landed on an album page with about twelve videos of varying lengths. I took out my notebook and pen, poised to take notes of anything that may be relevant.

The first video was a group of young women preparing for their night out, dressed to the nines in party dresses and high heels. They had started their night with some glasses of sparkling wine. They were in high spirits, talking over each other in their slightly intoxicated excitement. Then there were a few videos of the party, scenes of people chatting, drinking and dancing. In the sixth video, Alicja was dancing with another girl, she was an enthusiastic dancer and from my limited knowledge she looked like she was a natural on the dance floor. She looked happy, relaxed and full of vivacity. Looking at her I could see no hint that she was ready to leave behind her job, home and friends in Fife. It seemed she had not a care in the world, that her life was one long joyous party.

As I worked my way through the clips, I could see the slow deterioration of the guests as alcohol and other substances took control. The cinematography of the girl behind the camera also seemed to be suffering. The guests became more dishevelled and less co-ordinated, the camera shook more and struggled to focus on a subject.

The eleventh clip was shot from a window looking out on to the roof. There was a group of partygoers sitting on the slate, while one guy, filled with brewer's bravado, decided to walk across the pitch of the terraced roofs. The camera panned around to follow him as he climbed a chimney. As it moved back to the joker's audience, part of the street below outside the house could be seen on the right of the frame. I changed my focus from the crowd to the street. As I watched, a couple appeared in shot, walking along arm in arm. I rewound the video and watched again, now sure that my first impression was correct. It was Rupert Haines with Alicja on his arm.

The final video was again shot on the roof, this time with the blue lights of a fire engine flashing to illuminate the scene, which gave it a surreal strobing effect, like some outdoor night club. The group of guests had moved from the roof and the firefighters were arranging a ladder to remove the now fearful fool. He couldn't persuade his rubber legs to bring him down from his perch. There were lots of derisory comments from behind the camera as the others laughed at his predicament.

In the very corner of the shot, I could see Haines and Alicja standing on a street corner, in deep discussion about something. While the featured rescue continued to play out, Alicja suddenly buried her face in her hands. Haines seemed to try to placate her but she shunned him, throwing his hands off her. She then seemed to shout at him as he held his arms out wide as if pleading his case. As the firemen guided the drunken free runner from the chimney to ironic cheers from the assembled watchers behind the camera, Alicja ran away from Haines. The young man was apparently shouting after her but he didn't seem to be trying too hard.

At first I was shocked that Haines had told such a blatant lie. Then I was enraged at his arrogance. The frustration of the past couple of days, the lies, the distractions I had had to deal with and the thoughts of what may have happened to Alicja, all coursed through me. I had felt that Haines knew more than he was saying from the very first time I met him and now I had the proof.

When I calmed down a little I called Hero.

"Hi, Craig. did you get my mail?" he asked.

"Yes, that's what I'm calling you about. Rupert Haines had an argument with Alicja on the night of the party. They were together in two of the clips that were posted. I need to talk to him urgently, any idea where I might find him?"

He sounded a little shocked as he replied, "Man, eh, I'm not sure if he'll be in a lecture or not. He's got a place on Nelson Street I think, he might be there."

"Have you got a mobile number for him?" I'm sure that Hero could hear the desperation in my voice because it was certainly how I felt.

"No."

I then remembered that I had Haines number as he had sent me a text.

"It's OK, Hero. I've got it here."

He promised to get Gerard to send me the number of Haines' house in Nelson Street and asked me to let him know what happened. I assured him that I would and thanked him again for his help.

I sat with the dregs of my coffee, hoping that Gerard would send me the house number. When it hadn't arrived after ten minutes, I decided to go St Andrews anyway and hope to confront Haines with what I had discovered.

I packed everything into my rucksack, popped in to the room and kissed a barely awake Carol. She had been right, there was a break and now I had the evidence I needed to subject Haines to some rigorous questions.

The ride to St Andrews seemed interminably long but it was only 40 minutes.

I stepped away from the bike just as my phone vibrated.

Rupert's address, Regards Gerard.

I had parked the bike in the car park off Argyle Street. When I checked the route to Haines' flat I could tell that it wasn't far. I decided to walk there as I didn't know what parking would be like in Nelson Street. I marched quickly through the old town gates at the end of South Street and down Kiness Place towards my destination. I rang the door bell, his name was the only one on the door. He wasn't sharing this house with anyone, his family money allowed him to occupy a home without having to slum it with another student.

There was no reply and I pressed again, three times in quick succession, my irritation growing with every passing second. I turned away and began walking back and scanned my phone for the text from Haines. When I found the details I immediately dialled the number.

"Hello, Rupert Haines speaking."

"Rupert, it's Craig Campbell."

"Sorry, who?"

"Craig Campbell, we played putting together."

"Oh, Chubs' chum." He sounded like his usual nauseatingly, jaunty self.

"I need to speak to you urgently.'

"Whatever for old chap?"

"I need to speak to you about Alicja."

"I'm afraid I've told you all I know." The lie came easily to him.

The anger overtook me. "I know that's what you said but you're lying through your perfectly even teeth. I have proof you had an argument with Alicja. Hard evidence of the kind of argument that only lovers have. You better speak to me or you'll be speaking to the cops instead. I don't think your family name will be much use if you are facing charges of kidnapping or murder."

There was a long silence that I was about to fill before he said, "OK. I've got a class in five minutes, I'll meet you down near the castle at half past three."

I looked at my watch, it was nearly two o'clock.

I wasn't sure what to do but eventually I decided to give him a chance. If he didn't turn up, the case was over and Haines would be a problem that the police could handle. "Right, but if you don't appear I'll contact the police."

"It's OK. I'll be there." There was a distinct change in him, he almost sounded like a mature adult.

The call ended. I stood wondering what he would tell me or if he would even turn up. If he didn't, the case would be over for me.

*

The hour and a half I had to wait was like torture. I moved the bike down closer to the castle to give me something to do.

I walked around the nearby cathedral grounds looking at the gravestones. The once magnificent building was now a collection of disparate ruins. The ravages of time and the hands of the reformers had taken a heavy toll on what was one of the most significant religious sites in Scotland. The Augustinian monks began the construction of the Cathedral in 1160 but it wasn't until 1318 when Robert The Bruce was among those who attended the consecration that it was opened officially for worship. It then had to be rebuilt in the wake of a fire later that same century.

Long a place of Catholic pilgrimage, St Andrews became a target for those looking to change the Scots' relationship with their God. The Cathedral overlooked the sea like a bastion of humanity's defiance of all the forces nature could throw at it, and it was human hands that sundered the stones that neither the power of the wind nor the sea could shift. The end began in 1599 when John Knox, the reformation preacher, incited a crowd at St Andrews Parish Church to tear down the symbols of Catholicism. The Presbyterian clerics symbolically scrubbed away the old religion by tearing down the very stones the ancient cathedral was built from. Much of that stone went into building the town that surrounds the cathedral and the burial ground. The stones that remain hint at the awe that the structure once inspired.

St Rule's tower still stands at the east end of the ruins, a lonely reminder of a glorious age, defiantly resisting the depredations that had befallen the main building. I climbed the 151 steps to look out over the bay. The sun was shining but the North Sea was providing a chill, bracing wind that helped to clear my mental cobwebs. I tried to form an idea of how the conversation with Haines might go but I didn't know what he would say. Had he hurt her physically or emotionally? Had he killed her or had she run to escape him? I had no clue but I would soon find out.

I descended back into the graveyard and walked to where Young Tom Morris, one of golf's earliest champions, was buried. The grave listed the achievements that made him the Tiger Woods of his day.

At quarter past three, I walked back towards another one of the symbols of St Andrews' past trials. The castle stands proudly on a headland, defying the sea to do its worst. As with the Cathedral, the salt water had done little damage to the castle compared to its human attackers. There is now a visitor centre to welcome foreign guests where once they were discouraged and repelled by a moat, arrows and cannonballs.

I stood for a couple of minutes watching a seagull wrestle the remnants of a fish supper from a litter bin. It struggled with great determination before freeing its prize from the receptacle.

I looked along the road known as The Scores, and I could see Haines walking towards me. The swagger and arrogance seemed to have dissipated. He looked dispirited and diminished, his upper-class balloon of confidence deflated. He was carrying a sports bag which he let swing carelessly at his side.

"Mr Campbell." He nodded his head in a gesture of recognition.

"Mr Haines." I returned his greeting with equal formality.

"Shall we go up to the benches?" He indicated a couple of wooden seats on the path between the cathedral and the castle. We walked up to the first of them and sat down.

I began to present my evidence. "One of Hero's mates shot a video on the night of the party. Hero sent it to me and it proves you lied to me. You and Alicja were walking arm in arm, then you seemed to have a fight and she stormed off. What the hell really happened? Don't bullshit me this time because my patience has long gone." My tone was laced with a little Glaswegian gruffness to help him realise how serious I was.

He nodded and then to my surprise, he started to sob. Huge racking sobs, that came from somewhere deep in his being. A couple walking past stopped but I waved my hand to show that everything was OK. They continued to peer over their shoulders as they proceeded down the path.

He spoke very quietly, struggling to breathe due to the uncontrolled weeping. "I killed her."

"What?"

"It's my fault, she's dead and I killed her." His voice was barely a whisper as he held his head in his hands, drawing his legs towards him as if he was in pain. I was amazed at his sudden outburst of emotion, it was so uncharacteristic that it put me on the back foot.

"I think you'd better tell me the full story." My heart was racing, adrenaline fuelling my fear and excitement.

He calmed himself a little, although tears continued to fall. A deep breath allowed him to tell me the story.

"We met at a ball, around Easter time. She had been given some tickets by someone, I don't know who. She was there with her chum, Stefania. I thought Alicja looked beautiful and exotic. She wore a pale pink blouse and black trousers, her hair was perfect, she was captivating. I think I fell for her the minute I saw her.

We started seeing each other, quietly: I didn't want anyone to know. We went for walks and through to Kingsbarns for a drink. I avoided all the places that I might have bumped into fellow students. She was such fun, not like the dim dullards I normally go out with. I felt alive when I was with her."

"So what happened?"

The night of the party I think she thought that would be when we became a couple officially. But I kept my distance and I think she was confused.

When the nonsense started on the roof, I took the chance to go for a walk with her. She held my arm for a short time but I told her that nothing could come of us being together. I told her to find someone who could love her properly. She told me she loved me and pleaded with me but I dismissed her." He drew in a large gulp of air to get through the last few sentences.

"She was upset and then she got angry. We said a few things we shouldn't have and then she stormed away."

"Why the hell did you spin me that line about Michaels?"

"I couldn't let anyone know that we had a relationship."

"Why?"

A little of the old arrogance reared its ugly head. "People of my class have certain obligations. One of those is that we are expected to make a good marriage, to someone of similar background and education. I couldn't fall for a migrant farm worker. My family and friends would have ostracised me."

The little sympathy I had begun to feel was blown away by his shotgun of stupidity.

Astounded, I began to rant. "What? You're kidding. Listen to yourself. This is the 21st century, not the 19th. Who gives a damn what other people think if it made you happy? Did you tell Alicja this bollocks?"

"Not in so many words, no," he said with a touch of embarrassment.

"But she got the message, right?"

"I think so." He started to cry again.

I was no longer in the mood to offer any support, someone this stupid deserved everything that was coming to him. "Oh shut up, you arsehole. What happened after the argument?"

"I kept watching her as she walked away. She never looked back once."

The next question was difficult to ask. "So how did you kill her?"

"I drove her away and now she's gone, it's my fault."

"So you didn't harm her?"

He looked shocked as he realised what I had been thinking. "No. No. I would never hurt her, I loved her."

He withdrew again into an almost foetal ball.

"Is he all right?" An elderly woman out walking her dog had stopped. The dog sniffed curiously at Haines.

"He's fine. He's just realised that he made a huge mistake," I told her.

"Oh all right, if you're sure." She moved on, glancing back at Haines as she shuffled away.

"Look, we don't know for sure that something has happened to her. She may have decided to get away for a while to sort her head out. I need you to focus and think of anything she said or did that might give me a clue as to where she could have gone. I need the truth because your idiotic lie about Michaels cost me precious time."

He was distraught as the harsh reality of my words hit him in the solar plexus. "I don't know. She spoke about her home and her family a lot but nothing else. If she's not with them I don't know where she could be."

I felt like screaming. Every time I made a small stride forwards something would come to knock me back to where I had started.

"There was one thing, now that I think of it. As she walked away, Doctor Barclay got out of a car and seemed to be following her." A spark of hope had enlivened him a little.

"Barclay from biology?"

"Yes. He was having a fling with Alicja's friend, Alicja told me about it. She didn't approve of her being with a married man. She was quite adamant about it."

"Yes, I know about that. Barclay denied having seen her that night. Shit. It looks like he's another one that has been economical with the fucking truth." I shouted at him, furious with him and Barclay.

"Do you think he knows something about her disappearance? What did he have against her?"

"I don't know if it's him. He wouldn't want his wife hearing about his out-of-gown activities, maybe that was enough for him to kill the poor girl, who knows. I don't know anything about this case other than it's littered with fucking liars."

He looked shamefaced by my rebuke.

"I need to talk to him again."

I poked a finger at him. "You need to go and have a long think about what you want out of life. Live it for your family or your friends if money's all that matters to you but you'll be miserable. If you get a chance to be happy, even for a short time, grab it with both hands. Don't have regrets caused by other people's prejudices and outdated attitudes."

He nodded solemnly but I wasn't sure if my sounding off was anything more than hot air to him.

"I need to find Barclay, you better hope we can find Alicja alive."

He looked at me with fresh tears forming at the corner of his eyes. "I do. I do."

"I'll be in touch." I picked up my bag and headed back to the bike.

*

The journey to the Ocean Research Institute took only a few minutes.

The man on reception told me that Doctor Barclay had left for the day. My attempts to extract Barclay's home address proved fruitless.

Thwarted once again, I tried to think how I could get his address. I called Danielus' mobile phone to see if I could speak to Stefania but there was no reply.

A little deception would be required. I found a florist in St Andrews town centre and bought a substantial white bouquet consisting of carnations, roses and lilies. I had already found where the main biology school was and found my way to the main door, holding the flowers in the self-conscious way that men always do.

At the reception, I began my charade and slipped into my best Glaswegian accent.

"Ah've got flowers here fur Mrs Barclay."

The middle-aged receptionist looked at me as if I had brought a rotten smell into her presence.

"I beg your pardon."

"Flowers fur Mrs Barclay, fae her husband."

Her expression remained unimpressed.

"I'm afraid you've made a mistake, Doctor Barclay works in this department, not his wife."

"Well, this is the address ah've goat fur her."

"She's not here, you'll need to check your delivery slip again. I'm sure you'll find you've made a mistake."

I made a show of checking the notebook that I had slipped into my jacket.

"Naw, hen. Definitely here. He must've made the mistake. Will ah just leave them here?"

"Indeed you will not." You would have thought I had suggested leaving a pound of Stilton wrapped in my old socks.

"Look, ah cannae take them back. Ah've been in bother afore fur no' deliverin' stuff. Christ man, they'll sack me fur sure, even if it's no ma fault. Kin ye no' help me oot here?" I laid on my anguish with trowels of false misery.

The ice queen seemed to melt a little. Her tone was more conciliatory as she said, "I'm sorry but I don't know what I can do."

"Can you get this Doctor Barclay down, ah'll gie him the flowers and he can gie them tae his wife?"

"He's gone, I'm afraid."

"Oh man, whit am ah gonnae dae?" I laid the flowers on the desk, stood with my head in my hands and hoped the receptionist would feel sorry for me.

"Look, just this once I'll give you Mrs Barclay's address, as long as you don't tell anyone."

I smiled with genuine gratitude at her. "Aw thanks. Yir a gem, and no' a word tae anybody. Mum's the word." I tapped the side of my nose and gave her a knowing wink.

She looked up the address on the computer and passed me a handwritten note with the Barclays' address on it. I thanked her again and walked away.

There was a bounce in my step as I headed back to the Ducati. A young woman with a small child was passing and I offered her the flowers. She looked at me suspiciously. "Do I know you?"

"No, you don't, but we're doing a special promotion today to encourage people to buy more flowers. We're asking people to use their local florist rather than the internet and this is my last bouquet of the day. If you take it from me, I'll be finished and off home early."

She hesitated but eventually gave in, took the flowers and gifted me a dazzling smile in return. "Well, thank you."

"Remember use your local florist," I said brightly.

"I certainly will," she replied as she turned away.

The little girl waved a shy hand as I left them.

When I reached the bike I consulted my phone and calculated a route to the Barclay house. It didn't look as if it would be too difficult to find.

I rode up to the A915 until I found the junction for Canongate in the Craigtoun area of the town. Half a mile later I turned into a cul-de-sac, the Barclays home was on the corner on the right.

I lifted my bag from the storage box on the bike before I walked up a small flight of stairs and then the path to the front door.

The house looked as if it had been built in the eighties. It was a detached villa with white pebbledashed walls and a grey slate roof. There was an extensive, carefully managed lawn surrounding it, with bedding plants and tulips artistically placed to give a splash of spring colour. The whole garden looked well tended, as if someone had lavished a lot of love and care on it.

I rang the bell and watched through the frosted glass of the door as a shape approached. An attractive woman in her late forties opened it. I recognised her from the photo on Barclay's desk.

"Can I help you?" she smiled but with a quizzical look in her eyes.

"Mrs Barclay?"

"Yes."

"Is Doctor Barclay at home?"

"No, he's just popped out to the supermarket for some things."

"Would it be possible for me to wait for him?"

"What's this about?" she asked suspiciously.

I handed her my card as I said, "My name's Craig Campbell, I'm an insurance investigator. I'm working on an accident that happened a week past Saturday evening and we believe your husband may have witnessed it. There's some debate between the parties about what happened, so we're hoping that he may be able to clear some things up for us."

"I'm not sure."

"I can give you the phone number of a detective in Strathclyde Police who will vouch for me. I'm through from Glasgow for the day and it would be great if I could speak to your husband before I have to go back, it would save me a double trip."

I imagined that my bike leathers weren't inspiring any confidence in her, people have a certain impression of bikers and usually it's not a positive one.

"If I can speak to the detective that would help," She acquiesced.

I took out my phone and looked up Alex's work number in my contacts list. I pressed the button to begin the call, hoping that Alex would be on duty. I then passed the phone to the apprehensive woman.

"Her name is Detective Sergeant Alex Menzies."

She waited as the phone connected.

"Hello, can I speak to Detective Sergeant Menzies, please?"

I watched her and listened to one side of the conversation.

"Hello, yes. I've got a man here called Craig Campbell. He claims to be an insurance investigator."

There was a pause.

"He's about six feet tall, brown hair, brown eyes. He's wearing motorbike leathers."

Another short pause.

"He is, that's fine, thank you."

Mrs Barclay handed me the phone, "She wants to

speak to you."

I lifted the mobile to my ear in trepidation. My last conversation with Alex hadn't ended too amicably and I doubted that this little stunt would meet her approval.

"What the hell are you up to now?" There was a level of hostility that I hadn't heard from her before.

"I'm fine thanks. I'm just hoping to interview a witness." As Mrs Barclay was watching me, I had to make it appear as if all was well.

"If you drag me into something, this'll be the last conversation we have, I'm warning you."

"I'm sorry to have disturbed you, Alex, but Mrs Barclay needed some reassurance."

"I'm telling you Craig, this nonsense has to stop."

"That's fine, Alex. I'll catch up with you later in the week."

"Phone me later and let me know what this is all about."

"OK, will do. I promise. Bye."

The call was ended with no response from Alex. I was really regretting my previous rant.

"We were at university in Glasgow together," I said to Mrs Barclay by way of an explanation.

"Well you better come in, Mr Campbell."

I followed her through the hall into a spacious kitchen with an enormous window that looked out over the grandly landscaped back garden.

"Would you like a cup of tea, Mr Campbell?"

"Coffee would be better, if you have it."

"Certainly." She busied herself with a kettle, some coffee grounds and a cafétiere.

"You have a beautiful garden, Mrs Barclay."

She shone with pride as she said, "Why thank you. Are you a gardener yourself?"

"I'm afraid not. You couldn't meet anyone who was worse, if you were looking for an opposite of gardener in a dictionary it would say Craig Campbell. I have a talent for killing plants that would have me up as Britain's most wanted serial killer on Gardener's World."

She laughed, a bubbly infectious sound that made me smile in return. She was an incredibly attractive woman. Her black hair was shot with a little grey but still shone and bounced like a younger woman's. Her face reminded me of Audrey Hepburn, narrow and delicate, a classic beauty that men never tire of. She wore little make up because she knew she didn't need it. She was slim but not skinny, her clothes were both casual and stylish, they hung perfectly from her frame in a way a designer would love. I wondered why her husband felt the need to chase other women when he had someone like this to come home to.

"My name is Grace. Mrs Barclay seems very formal."

"Craig," I made a little bow with my head. "Pleased to meet you Grace."

She laughed again.

"Frank never mentioned anything about an accident."

"No one was hurt but the company I represent are concerned that their client isn't telling the truth about what happened and they want to know more. This guy apparently has a bit of a history of claims and they think that the accident may have been staged between him and the other party." Lying had become an all too easy habit for me since last December.

"Some people will try anything, won't they?" she said.

"You wouldn't believe some of the things that I've seen, Grace."

We sat at the kitchen table with our coffee as I told her some of the swindles that I had investigated through the years, the chancers and the con men who were never quite intelligent enough to see their schemes through.

"That's not to say the insurance companies are angels. Some of them will do anything to stop paying out, protect the share holders at all costs."

"No, I suppose not."

I decided to change the subject. "How long have you and Doctor Barclay been together?"

"We met at uni, twenty years ago now. We fell in love and married as soon as I was finished my studies. I was pregnant within a year and became a housewife while Frank worked on his doctorate. It was hard at first but we've had a good life."

"How many children do you have?"

"Two. Jonathan and Francis. Jonathan's down at Cambridge and Francis is at MIT in the States."

"Clever lads. You must be very proud of them and of course you must miss them?"

"Yes, the house is too big for the two of us but I love the garden so much, I couldn't bear to move. I have worked on it for ten years and it's finally how I want it."

We continued chatting and after half an hour I heard a key in the front door.

"I couldn't get the usual olive oil..." Doctor Barclay's eyes betrayed his shock at seeing me. He carried two bags of shopping through and placed them on the worktop in the kitchen.

"This is Craig, he's an insurance investigator. He thinks you might be able to help him about an accident that you might have witnessed." Mrs Barclay was smiling broadly as she added, "We've been having an interesting discussion about the lies people tell."

I almost laughed as Barclay fired an angry stare in my direction, a look that was out of his wife's sightline. I was sure that lies were probably the one subject the good Doctor would have preferred to have avoided.

"Yes, I need some help about the incident that occurred a week past Saturday."

His face was a portrait of conflicting emotion, fear and anger competing for ascendancy, a portrait of a man caught in a web of lies that was beginning to get sticky. He began to put the shopping away but Mrs Barclay insisted that she would do it and that he should speak to me.

"We'll go through to the lounge."

"Would you like some more coffee, Craig?" Mrs Barclay asked, oblivious of her husband's feelings towards me.

"I'm sure he's very busy." Barclay said emphatically.

"No, I'm fine. Another coffee would be great." I was enjoying his discomfort and was hoping to put it to good use when I spoke to him.

I followed the now enraged Doctor into the lounge at the front of the house. He closed the door behind him to ensure that Grace didn't hear anything of our conversation.

The lounge was decorated with muted pastel pink walls, a dusky pink carpet and a collection of antique furniture. There were family photographs on nearly every surface, oil and watercolour paintings of flowers graced the walls. I sat in an armchair as Barclay sat opposite on a settee.

"What the hell are you playing at?" he asked furiously through gritted teeth.

"I realise you are a practiced liar but I've caught you out on this one." I was removing my recorder, notepad and pen from my bag as I spoke.

"What the hell are you talking about?"

"I know you spoke to Alicja in person that night. There was a witness."

"What witness?" The second word was delivered with as much contempt and sarcasm as he could muster.

"Someone saw you with Alicja. She was very upset, I want to know what happened next."

He was about to answer when the lounge door swung open and Mrs Barclay delivered the coffee with a plate piled high with a selection of biscuits.

"Thank you, Grace. You're very kind," I said, and was rewarded with her stunning smile. Barclay noticed and it added jealousy to his already considerable list of negative emotions.

When Grace had gone, he closed the door again.

"What's you're fucking game?" He was too polite for the swear word to carry the weight that he hoped.

"Game? There's no game. There is a young woman whose life might be in danger or worse: there's a lying, cheating bastard who has prevented me from making any progress in finding her and I have to wonder why. There's no game."

"You've got some balls coming here. If Grace finds out what's been happening, our marriage will be over. That's why I lied."

"As far as Grace goes you don't deserve her but that's not my call. Don't worry, I didn't say anything that would give your dirty little secret away."

"What was that stuff about lies then?"

"We were talking about false insurance claims, if you must know. Now are you going to tell me what happened or am I going to tell the police what I know and let them interview you?"

He reacted with shock at my suggestion. "Look, I had nothing to do with that girl disappearing, you have to believe me."

"Convince me." I sipped the coffee and lifted a piece of shortbread from the plate.

"I did see her that night. I knew she and Stefania were supposed to go to a party but I didn't know the exact address, just the street name. I arrived about eleven, and parked at the end of the street. There was some commotion on the roof and I realised which house the party was in. A fire engine arrived and it all got a bit chaotic.

"Alicja appeared with one of the students, I don't know his name, he's not in any of my classes. They seemed OK at first, just strolling and chatting. Then there was some kind of argument. She was shouting at him but I couldn't hear what was said. He was trying to calm her down but she was very upset. She left him behind and stormed past my car. I got out and went after her.

When I caught up with her, she was crying, her make up was running, black tears were streaming down her face.

I was going to challenge her about Stefania, tell her that it was none of her business, but when I saw the mess she was in I decided against it. I told her who I was and I asked her if she needed a lift anywhere but she reacted angrily, swore at me and told me to go away."

I noted the details but the information didn't really help me.

"Is there anything else you can tell me?"

"By the time I had turned the car to drive away, she was walking down the street with another girl that had come from the party. I think she was having a smoke outside the house when the argument happened but I'm not sure."

"Can you describe her?"

"About the same height as Alicja, dark hair, thin. But I didn't get a good look at her under the street lights. Anyway, she was walking with this girl who seemed to be consoling her and just as I drove passed a car stopped beside them."

"A car? Do you know what make or model?"

"It was a four-wheel-drive thing. A Toyota or Land Rover maybe."

I picked up my phone and found the photo of Christina, the woman Michaels had killed.

"Could this have been the girl?"

"It could be but I didn't get a good look at her."

"What about the car, what colour was it?"

"I'm not sure but it might have been blue or

green, hard to tell in the yellow of the street lights."

"OK, thanks, but I wish you had told me this the first time I spoke to you."

There seemed little remorse in him, as if protecting his own tawdry secrets was more important to him than the life of a young woman.

I packed away my things in the bag. I was angry enough to tell Grace the truth about her scumbag husband and walk away but it would probably do her more harm than good. She didn't deserve the way he treated her but it wasn't up to me to make her realise that.

"What will I tell Grace?" he asked as I walked to the lounge door.

"I'm pretty sure you'll be able to think of something, you're probably pretty good at lying and deceiving her after all these years."

I said my farewell to Mrs Barclay, who offered me dinner, which I politely declined. Barclay walked me to the front door, not even saying goodbye as he closed the door firmly behind me.

I finally had a lead. Bennett drove a Land Rover, now I had to find him.

*

As I was putting the bag back into the luggage box on the bike, my phone rang. I looked at the display; it was Ruta's number.

"Hello, Craig Campbell."

"Meester Campbell, it is Ruta."

"Hi, Ruta."

"I have looked at journal for you. Do you want to hear now?" she asked.

"Yes, yes of course." The more information I had the better it would be.

"I don't know what will help."

"Just give me a summary from the start if you don't mind."

"OK. She began writing journal at home in Poland. There is some things about her Papa. He is unwell and she is worried about leaving him.

"She comes to Scotland, there is much about being scared of new country. After a month she is happier, I think. She writes about Danielus being nice to her but she does not like boss. One day she said that she hates boss and is thinking of going home. Danielus tells her it is OK, that she must ignore him for her family's sake.

There is part where she meets boy called Rupert. I think he is boyfriend."

I interrupted her. "Well, sort of. I found out about it earlier today."

"She say that diary is only one she can tell. It is secret."

"OK. Anything else?"

I could hear her flicking through pages of the book. "Here, she write that Stefania is being stupid or foolish maybe. She is with married man, Alicja thinks he is using Stefania. Her writing is angry."

"Yes, I've just spoken to the married man, he's another one that's been lying to me, like almost every other person involved in this. Is there any more, any sign she was in trouble or was thinking of going home?" I was keen to find something to tie Bennett to Alicja.

More pages were turned. "Two weeks ago she writes this: 'Boss man was strange today. He wanted me to go somewhere with him but I am scared. He is behaving differently, he called me by another girl's name. I said I would not go and he grabbed me but I managed to pull away.'"

Everything was pointing to Bennett and the need to get my hands on him grew with every second.

"Is there anything else, Ruta? Did Alicja have any other trouble with her boss?"

"No, she write about the man she loved but nothing else about this boss."

"OK, thank you for doing that."

"I hope it helps."

"I think it has, I think it's been a big help."

"I heard about Michaels. They say the police arrest him. He was the one who killed Christina?"

"It looks that way. It might mean you are out of work, what will you do?"

"Maybe it is time I go home. Start again, finish my college and see what happens." A weight seemed to have lifted from her by the simple act of telling me. I was pleased for her and hoped that her future would be brighter.

"I think that sounds like a good plan Ruta. Good luck."

"Thank you and goodbye Meester Campbell."

"Bye Ruta, and thanks again."

*

The clock on my phone told me that it was six-thirty. I decided to try Danielus to see if Bennett was still at work, or if he knew where I might find Bennett.

Danielus answered the call with hope in his voice.

"Hello, Craig. Have you any news?"

"I may have made some progress but I need to check one or two things. Is Bennett still at the farm?"

"No, he has gone. He will be drinking by now. He always goes to the pub when he finishes work."

"In St Andrews?"

"Yes, usually. Some times he goes to Cupar but normally St Andrews."

"You wouldn't know which one would you?" I asked more in hope than expectation.

"No, I'm afraid not."

"Where does he live? Do you know?"

"I think it is called Kinnessburn Road, close to town centre. I don't know the number."

"That's OK, I'll find him."

"Is it him? Is he the one that has harmed her?" he asked anxiously.

"I don't know for sure yet but I'll let you know, I promise."

"OK, bye."

I hung up and climbed aboard the Ducati. I rode back in to town, weaving through the traffic and avoiding the potholes. I parked at the west end of South Street as a large number of the pubs in St Andrews were situated somewhere along its length. I started in the Drouthy Neebors, searching the nooks and crannies, peering at people who regarded me with curious looks in return, but Bennett was nowhere to be seen.

I went through the same procedure, with the same reaction from the patrons, in another three or four pubs before finding him in a booth at the back of the Criterion. An ale house since the middle of the 19th century, it's a friendly bar, popular with locals and tourists alike. The wood-panelled walls, little booths and hand-pumped ales gave it a very tradi- tional Scottish pub atmosphere.

There were three empty pint glasses in front of Bennett and his eyes were already slightly glazed as he looked up at me.

"Look who it is, Craig fuckin' Campbell. Defender of the innocent and general pain in the fuckin' arse." He laughed at his statement, a drunken guffaw. "Whit the fuck dae ye want noo?" he grunted.

I slid in opposite him. The earthy smell of farm dirt, combined with his own individual stench wafted over me like a noxious gas.

"I want you to tell me what you've done with the girl." I kept my voice level and quiet, trying to stop him from erupting into a fury or attracting the attention of the other customers. It didn't work.

"How many times dae ah need tae tell ye, ah don't know where the stupid cow is? Ur ye fuckin' thick or somethin'? You keep fuckin' hasslin' me, why don't ye find the prick that did it? Ah think you must fancy me or somethin'. You a homo tae?" He laughed again.

Struggling to keep my own composure, I said, "I've got a witness who saw your car stop next to Alicja and her friend that Saturday night. She wrote in her diary that you were pestering her. Now what the hell have you done with her?" I was losing the battle to stay calm.

His face was a study in confusion and shock. "Me? Ah never went near her, she's a lying cow."

"What about the witness?"

"It wisnae me, ah tell ye. When ah finish work ah drive tae the hoose and leave the motor there, ken. Ah kin walk tae the pub and walk back. Ah wis in here that Saturday. Billy'll tell ye." He gestured towards the barman, "Billy, gonnae come here a minute?"

The barman walked over. He was in his early twenties, thin with limbs like branches of a young tree. He wore glasses and his fair hair was already well receded.

"Billy, gonnae tell this arsehole that ah wis here aw night on the Saturday that wee Kenny goat the

242

four numbers up on the lottery? The night he bought everybody a round."

The barman nodded as he said, "That was a week past Saturday wasn't it? Aye, you were here and had a good bucket in you. Mind you that could be any Saturday." He smiled at Bennett.

"But aye, I remember that day, wee Kenny had spent his winnings in one round." He confirmed Bennett's story.

"Ta, Billy. See ah tellt ye, ah could hardly walk, never mind drive a fuckin' motor."

I was confused, I was so sure that it was him. "Sorry, but what about the stuff she wrote in her diary?"

"No me. Whit did she say exactly?" He leaned forward as if he was interested in what I had to tell him: I was engulfed in a mixture of beery breath with under tones of halitosis and that faint hint of weed that I had detected the previous day.

"She said that she had been hassled by her boss. She didn't mention any names but I assumed that it must be you."

"How? Cause you looked at me and decided ah must be guilty. Ye're a fanny. Maybe it was another boss she wis talkin' aboot."

"Like who?"

He seemed a little reluctant to tell me but eventually he said, "Colin."

Shocked, I asked, "Colin, what makes you say

that?"

"Ah'm gonnae tell ye somethin' that ah've no told anybody before. It's aboot Bosnia and whit happened tae Colin. But ye never heard this fae me, awright?"

I wasn't sure how it would be relevant but if he thought it was important, I was willing to listen.

"OK."

"We wur sent tae Bosnia in ninety three as part o' the peace keepin' force. The whole country wiz fucked up beyond belief. We were based in Vitez but we hud tae go tae Sarajevo as part o' oor duties.

"Anyway, it was oor squad's turn fur Sarajevo. It wis aboot the maist screwed-up place ye'll ever see. The Serbs were bombin' the shit oot it. Ye didnae ken who wis friendly and who wis the enemy when ye were oan patrol. Folk couldnae walk alang some o' the streets withoot some arsehole wi' a gun takin' a pot shot at them. Sniper alley they cawd the main road, ken?"

"I remember the news reports and studying it in Modern Studies at school."

"Well the news didnae ken the half o' it. It wis a tough place tae be awright. A few o' the locals would help oot roon the camp fur some cash and food. There wis this lassie, Adrijana wis her name. She worked in the kitchen some times. She wis a pretty decent lookin' bird, skinny but fit, nice face. Anyhow, Colin started tae talk tae her, getting tae ken her a bit better. She wanted tae learn English, so she could

244

get away fae that place aw the gither. So Colin would help her wi' her studies when he wisnae oan duty, getting her tae read books we hud in camp. She wis learnin' English reading John Grisham and shit like that.

"She wis born in Bosnia but wis an ethnic Serb, if ye ken whit ah mean. At the start o' aw the troubles, when she wis a bit younger, she'd seen her Da' shoot her uncle in the heid. The uncle was a Bosnian and had been merried tae Adrijana's Serbian auntie fur aboot ten years or somethin'. Her Da' just decided tae kill the uncle wan day, oot the blue, he jist went fuckin' mental. The lassie wis freaked oot by it and ran away fae her Ma and Da. She heard later that a Serbian death squad had killed her auntie as a traitor, that wis aboot a month efter she left.

"Colin goat tae ken aw this stuff when he wis teachin' her, like. He fell fur her big style cos she wis a nice person, despite whit she'd been through. She seemed tae faw fur him an' aw. They talked aboot how he could get her back tae Scotland, start a new life the gither." His whole demeanour had changed from the obnoxious clown that I'd come to know and hate.

"No long afore we were due tae go back tae Vitez, we opened the camp gates wan mornin' tae find Adrijana's body dumped ootside. Wan o' the guys went tae get Colin and he came rushin' oot tae see her. She had been shot four times, baith o' her nipples had been cut aff, she'd been violated wi' a knife or a sword and had baith hauns cut aff. The medics reckoned she'd been alive when maist it wis done tae her, tortured, like. They reckon that she was dumped as a warnin' fae the Serbian militia. They wur tryin' tae stoap the locals workin' wi' us.

"Colin wis devastated. He held her in his erms until the medics took her away. We wur aw worried aboot him but he said nothin' aboot her efter that, no even tae me. It wis like she never existed."

The cynical, hard man act gone, he bowed his head in remembrance as he relived the trauma.

"It's a horrible story but I don't understand what it has to do with Alicja."

"She's Adrijana's double. Ah mean, double. The minute ah saw her, ah thought she wis like a ghost. I heard Colin caw her Adrijana wance or twice. He's never spoke aboot whit happened but maybe somethin' happened when Alicja arrived. Maybe it aw came rushin' back, maybe the fact he kept it aw tae himsel' has finally caught up wi' him. Ah dinnae ken but if anybody hassled her it wis probably him."

"Alicja mentioned in the journal that he had called her by a different name, that he seemed a bit strange."

"Look, he's ma mate, ah don't want tae talk bad aboot him, but that kind o' thing can scar a guy, ken. Disnae matter how good a person ye ur before ye go tae a place like Bosnia, yir a different man when ye get back."

"I know and I hope what we're both thinking is wrong but I need to look into it. Do you think he could have taken her?"

"Ah don't know but ah know whit combat kin dae tae the maist sane o' men. It fucks up yir view o' the world, the things ye see, the things ye dae, they poison ye fur ever."

"Is there anything else that might have sparked this? I mean is it only how Alicja looks or could there be something else?"

"It must be roon aboot this time o' year that Adrijana wis killt. Maybe the anniversary but ah cannae be sure, ken?"

I nodded. Could this be enough to make Colin Rose harm a girl he hardly knew? I'm no psychologist but I had seen and read enough about post traumatic stress to know that it can affect people in different ways; the scars running deep through a person's life and tormenting them long after they leave the combat zone.

"Do you think he would have killed her or kidnapped her?"

"Ah dinnae ken. Who kens whit somebody that confused could dae? Maybe kidnap, keep her tae himsel', keep her safe by his way o' thinkin'."

"Where would he take her if he had kidnapped her?"

He considered my question. "No sure. Naewhere oan the ferm, too many folk."

"What about the other farm the Roses bought recently? Are there people working there?"

"Oot in the fields but there's naebody stayin' in the auld ferm buildin's, ah don't think. Could be there ah suppose."

"Right, can you give me directions?"

"Aye, sure. Gies a bit o' paper an' a pen."

I passed him my notebook and pen, which he used to create a sketched map of how to get to the old Strawberry Hill Farm.

When he was finished the directions he handed back both items.

"Look, ah ken ah've been an arse. Sometimes life ootside the army's been too tough. Ah'm shite at coping, angry wi everybody and everythin', ken. But ah widnae hurt anybody, honest. Definitely no a lassie.

I hope she's aw right, cos he'll be in a shitload o' trouble if she's no, right?"

"If it's him he'll need help but the police will definitely want to talk to him."

"Shite. This is totally fucked up." He took a long draw on his pint of beer.

"I need you to keep quiet about this. He needs to be caught or God knows where this'll end. You can't warn him that I'm coming." I tried to ensure that he understood that the best thing to do for his friend was to let this come to an end.

"Ah ken, ah ken." He looked abject as I stood up.

"Make sure he disnae hurt himsel' or anybody else, wid ye?" he asked sincerely.

"I'll do everything I can." It was as much as I could offer as I had no idea how it would work out.

We parted with Bennett staring at the remains of his pint, lost in his own thoughts.

I ran as fast as I could to my bike, desperate to get to the Strawberry Hill Farm quickly, hoping that I wouldn't be too late.

*

The road seemed never ending as I pushed the bike as hard as I dared. Although it felt like hours, within fifteen minutes I was pulling in to the deserted farm yard.

An anvil of dark purple cloud was building up out on the North Sea and the light had diminished to a twilight glimmer. I could see the rain tumbling from the cloud in dense streaks and it would be over the farm within a few minutes.

I opened my luggage box and retrieved the torch I always carried.

The farm house was a large structure, constructed of the same grey stone that characterised the majority of the buildings in the St Andrews area. There were no curtains on the windows and the wooden frames looked as if they hadn't been painted in years. The whole place had a neglected and forgotten air, as if the residents had left long before the farm had been bought by the Roses.

I walked to the door. The wood was cracked and dry, faded to a silvery grey colour. I tried to open it but it was locked. Desperate to get inside, I had no other choice but to kick it open. It took three attempts before the frame gave way and the door flew wide with loud crack which reverberated across the empty farmyard.

I switched the torch on to illuminate the dark interior. I was in the kitchen. A large country-style table sat abandoned in the middle of the floor, three chairs sitting waiting for diners who would never come. As the cone of light traversed the surfaces I could see that everything else seemed to have been removed, any trace of the previous life of the house gone, as if the only residents the house had ever had were spiders and mice. The dust on the floor had been disturbed recently by a two-legged guest, footprints were clearly visible and there were four voids in the dirt where another chair's legs would have been.

In the hall, to the left of the internal kitchen door, there was another room. Moving stealthily, the creepy atmosphere of the house getting to me, I walked into the vacated space. Floorboards creaked a complaint and I could hear the scurrying of little feet running to escape the beam of my torch. The room had been cleaned out. The only remnants of the pre-vious owners were the gaps in the colour of the wall-paper where pictures had once hung and a rectangu-lar space on the floor where a rug had once resided.

Another door at the far end of the room led me

back into the hall, close to the front door and the bottom of the stairs. There was another room directly opposite but it was similarly untouched and empty.

I stepped cautiously on to the stair as a flash of lightning lit the house followed by a loud crash of thunder. It took me a few seconds to still my heart again before I could continue my climb.

There were three bedrooms and a bathroom on the upper floor but none of them showed any sign that anyone had visited them in a while. From one of the windows at the back of the house I spotted another building about a hundred yards away from the main farm complex.

As I walked back down the stairs I could hear the rain begin to patter on the roof, an insistent drumbeat that increased in volume and speed.

Back in the hall, I turned towards the kitchen. On the left, below the stairs, I noticed another door. I expected it to be a cupboard but it was another set of steps, leading into a basement. My stomach flipped and my heart began to pound. My legs turned to jelly and it was difficult to force them to carry me down into the darkness.

The concrete steps made no sound as I descended. The light from my torch shook in time to the trembling movements of my hand.

At the bottom I began to move the light across the room but there was nothing of any consequence. I let out a long sigh of relief. I had been holding my breath all the way down without even realising it.

251

The cellar smelled vaguely of washing powder and fabric softener, I presumed that the previous owners had used it as an utility room.

I ascended the steps much more quickly than I had crept down them.

By the time I stepped out of the back door into the yard the rain was pouring down so hard it looked like Hollywood rain. My hair was soaked by the time I had covered the short distance to a block of stables at the side of the main farm house.

All of the stables smelled of manure and were unlocked, deserted and bereft of anything that would help me. A barn next to the stables was equally useless; a few bales of straw were the only things to be seen. I began to doubt my own theory of what had happened. I had been wrong so many times already with this case.

Soaked and beginning to feel despondent, I remembered the outbuilding I had seen from the window.

I trudged through the rapidly forming mud, which sucked at my boots, up a hill to what looked like a big shed or garage. The lightning raced across the sky, highlighting a copse of trees behind the building.

The large double doors were closed tightly, a brand new lock holding them shut. Suddenly I knew I was right, there was something here. The wood of the shed had not seen a coat of paint or varnish in a long time. The timber was rotting in places, dry and brittle in others. I ran around the building to the trees, my torch searching the ground for a branch of a decent size.

After a couple of minutes I found what I was looking for. It was a good stout piece of wood, narrow at one end where it had broken from the tree.

Back at the lock, I managed to get the tree branch between the doors, close to where the bolt held them together. I worked at trying to loosen the bolt from the fragile, disintegrating wood of the door. The rain continued to batter down, making my lever slippery, but eventually, after minutes of effort and a lot of swearing, there was a satisfying report as the wood split and the bolt came away.

I threw the branch away and eased the door opened. The foetid air rushed out to meet me. There was a distinctive aroma of lubricating oil, with under-tones of rotting wood and something else: another altogether more ominous odour.

After closing the door behind me, I moved the torch from left to right and it illuminated a figure in the centre of room. I rushed over to where Alicja was sitting on the fourth chair from the kitchen, with cable ties bonding her to it and holding her firmly in place.

Her head was lolling to one side. The dress she had worn to the party was torn open, her torso exposed. Her underwear had been removed, and there were four distinct marks across her chest that looked like burns, possibly from a cigarette lighter from a car. The top of both her nipples had been bleeding; little rivers of dried blood painted her breasts. It looked like Rose had begun to cut them and then stopped. As I reached to test for a pulse I noticed the faintest rise and fall of her chest as she pulled in a weak breath through the gag of fabric that was obstructing her mouth. I closed her dress, trying to give back a little of the dignity that had been ripped from her.

I shone the torch around the building, looking for something to cut her free. There was a collection of rusting tools at the back on a dusty work bench. A pair of ancient pliers was the best implement I could find.

As I swung around to return to help Alicja, I saw another figure, apparently floating in a pool of blood. The dark skin told me who it was before I got close. George had been blasted with a shotgun at close range. His broken body was the source of the foreboding aroma of death and decay I had noticed on entering the room. He had been left to bleed out like some farm pest casually tossed aside. The whites of his eyes contrasted with his dark skin, as he stared into the bleak emptiness. I leaned over and closed his eyelids, a brief poignant thought for his family back home in Ghana crossed my mind. He had obviously witnessed something, tried to intervene and had died for his compassion.

My stomach heaved and it was all I could do to stop myself from vomiting my abhorrence. There was nothing more I could do for him but Alicja still needed me.

As I moved towards her I noticed the bizarre tableau that surrounded her. There were flowers, some decaying, some still alive with colour. The small toy bears that had occupied her pillow in the caravan now sat beside the chair. Her handbag lay close to her, the contents carelessly strewn across the floor. There were pieces of jewellery and boxes of chocolates, all laid out like some tribute to a goddess. It was as if she was the centrepiece of some hellish altar, the worship of an idol broken by her extremely disturbed follower.

The pliers were too far gone to be of any use, the blades were blunt and refused to make the slightest impression on the tough plastic of the ties. As I struggled to free her, she opened her eyes. The sheer terror in them, a vision of a haunted soul, will live with me for the rest of eternity. She began to thrash about, trying to escape her bonds.

"Alicja, it's OK. My name's Craig Campbell. Danielus asked me to help you. Do you understand?" I removed the gag.

Her lips were dry and cracked, she tried to talk in Polish but her voice croaked and rasped due to the lack of moisture. I couldn't understand what she was saying. She tried again but the only word I could understand was George.

"I'm sorry, Alicja but George is dead."

She stopped, her face suddenly devoid of expression. She fell silent again. The agony of the past few days and the death of her friend pushed her somewhere beyond emotion, back to the safety of her own internal defences.

"I have to get you out of this chair. I want to tip it on its side to see if I can break the legs. I don't want to hurt you, do you understand?"

She nodded a weak agreement.

As gently as I could, I manoeuvred the chair on to its side. I kicked at the back leg, earning a groan from Alicja.

"I'm sorry."

Another couple of tries and the leg was detached from the seat. After some considerable effort I liberated Alicja's arms, although they were still held together by the plastic tie.

With the structure of the chair weakened it was easier to remove the other legs and before long she lay with her legs free in the centre of her sinister accolades.

"Can you stand?"

She made an attempt to get to her feet but the captivity had weakened her too severely. I reached for her and was about to help her up when I heard a noise from outside that sounded like a gun. I couldn't be sure in the cacophony of rain and thunder but the hairs on the back of my neck stood on end.

Once again I bent to pick up Alicja, precisely at the moment a series of holes appeared in the door, a spray of shotgun pellets having cut through the rotting wood with the ease of a logger's saw through an ancient pine.

"You Serbian bastards better leave her alone."

Colin Rose's voice penetrated into every corner of the building. Alicja squealed, a response laced with terror, she scrambled to move away from the noise.

"You're not getting her again. Adrijana is mine."

Alicja's, her panic rising, shuffled backwards away from the door, away from her torturer, her face ribboned with tears.

I tried to calm her down but she was too far into the darkest recesses of her mind to care what I said.

Another shot rang out and punctured another, more substantial hole in the door.

"You better come out or I'll come in there and finish you." Rose's voice was now almost robotic, inhumanly cold, his own past now dominating him.

Staying low I picked up the torch, being careful to keep it facing the rear of the building. I don't know what I hoped to find but there was nothing to combat a gun. Somehow I had to get Alicja out of the building. We were easy targets, trapped as we were.

On the right, close to the back of the building, I could see some light. The dim twilight of the rain-drenched evening was visible through some particularly distressed boards. I grabbed a rusting hammer and began to work at the wood with the claw end, hoping to loosen the structure and create an exit.

Another shot rang out and some of the pellets hit something metallic, causing a ringing sound and producing a minor fireworks show of sparks. Some of the sparks must have landed on paper or rags because suddenly flames began to lick up the rear wall. My own panic was climbing but it was a small pebble on a great beach compared to Alicja's endless screaming. She grabbed my leg, I could feel her nails on my calf, even through my bike leathers.

Some of the boards were freeing up, bits of the wood crumbling while others held together with surprising strength. All the while Alicja continued to scream. Her horror was the constant soundtrack to our own living hell.

By now the flames were beginning to make their way to the left and the right of their original ignition point. The heat intensified as smoke began to sting my eyes.

The inside of the shed was now fully lit. George's body, the unholy altar and a large drum of heavy engine lubricant were all clearly visible. I dreaded to think what would happen if the flames reached the drum if it was full.

"Adrijana, come out, darling. I'll look after you. I won't let those Serbian bastards hurt you again." He pleaded and cajoled but there was always a hint of madness behind everything he said.

This entreaty was followed by another shot, a different sound, a hand gun I thought.

Finally, I had created enough space to get us both through and out to safety. I prised Alicja's fingers from my leg and tried to lift her from below my legs but she was a dead weight, frozen by her terror. It took a couple of attempts to get her securely in a fireman's lift grip. I squeezed through the door, successfully extricating my arm from a large splinter of wood. When we were out in the rain, Alicja's screaming stopped suddenly, as if the water had acted as a switch. I walked as quickly as I could with my fragile bundle to the copse of trees. I walked in about ten feet or so and laid her on the ground.

"Please Alicja, you need to stay quiet. I need to distract Colin until help arrives. Please, you need to understand." I begged that she would obey.

She nodded.

"Stay here, stay still and stay quiet," I whispered.

I reached for the torch and realised I had laid it down beside the exit that I had created in the shed. By now the back wall was engulfed in flames, the rain not enough to slow their destructive power. I ran back, reached through the hole and switched off the light before I picked it up. I then ran back to the woods, my legs driving me forwards despite the paralysing effect the gun fire was having on my brain. I was running on instinct alone. As the lightning continued to crackle and the thunder boomed like shells falling on a battlefield, I had a sudden thought of how this was almost like a combat zone. I noticed a low dry stone wall to the left of the trees and moved towards it.

The flames in the shed suddenly blossomed further across the structure. Rose had opened the door and let more oxygen fuel the flames. He was calling Adrijana's name, believing his dead lover to be caught in the inferno. He fired the gun a few more times as if he was trying to beat the blaze back with his bullets.

I was crouched behind the wall and while he was occupied inside, I pulled my phone from my pocket and dialled 999.

"Emergency services, which service do you require?"

"All three to Strawberry Hill Farm about five miles outside St Andrews. There is an armed man and an injured girl, please hurry."

"Can you tell me some more, sir?"

"Look, he's got at least two guns, please send help now!"

"Can you confirm that address for me, sir."

"Fuck, it's Strawberry Hill Farm about five miles outside St Andrews."

I ended the call as Rose walked out of the shed, beaten back by the heat and the smoke. I hoped they would get the message and not think I was some kind of nut.

"You fucking bastards, I'll kill every one of you," Rose screamed into the night air with the ferocity of a demon.

I scrambled to the right, staying as low as I could behind the stone wall. When I had cleared the trees by about fifty yards, I briefly lit the torch to attract the madman's attention.

"I fucking see you. I'll kill you, you murderous bastard." He was out of control, firing the gun another couple of times in my general direction. One of the bullets hit the wall and shards of stone stung my face. My heart was thumping in my chest, my legs were sapped of strength, my own combat stress was almost completely debilitating. Despite that, I knew I had to keep him away from Alicja until help arrived.

I edged further away from the trees and flashed the torch again. It provoked the same response, another unintelligible rant and two shots fired in my general direction. I could see by the light of the now substantial conflagration that he had moved closer to me.

Suddenly there was an enormous explosion. A mushroom of bright red flame interspersed with clouds of dense black smoke rose from the shed like a mythical beast had been summoned from the depths of hell. Sizeable pieces of charred and burning wood were thrown in all directions. The force of the blast knocked Rose to one side but he was up on his feet again before I could react.

Some of the burning wood had been catapulted into the trees. I was now caught in a dilemma: go and check on Alicja or keep Rose away from her. Nothing made sense, any decision I took could be the wrong one.

"Colin, listen, it's Craig Campbell. I'm not a Serbian death squad and the girl you abducted isn't Adrijana. Her name is Alicja."

I could see him trying to pinpoint where my voice was coming from. "Very good. Almost had me convinced you were a Scot there but I can hear that Serbian accent. I know what you did to Adrijana, you're a shower of fuckin' psychos." His voice made a gravelly sound, as if his throat had been shredded by his screaming.

With no weapons other than my voice to resist him, I decided to try to talk him out of wherever his disorientated mind had taken him. "If you know what happened to her, you must know she's dead. If that's true, who was the girl in the shed?"

There was a pause before he replied, "What? Stop trying to confuse me, come out where I can see you, come out and fight like a real soldier rather than skulking away hiding behind kids and women. Come out, you evil bastard."

Another three shots pinged the wall directly in front of me, shrapnel, stone and dust covered me.

I scurried about ten yards nearer to the woods. The rain had eased a little and the thunder seemed more distant than it had been. I listened in the hope of hearing the emergency vehicle sirens but there was nothing. I didn't know how long the police would take to get to me and I imagined they would have to be the first here to secure the scene.

"Colin, you need to listen to me. The war is long over, you're at home in Fife, this is not Bosnia. All that happened seventeen years ago. The girl you kidnapped is not Adrijana. You need help, Colin. Please, you have to listen to me."

Another two shots but thankfully they were well wide of their target.

"You're ill, Colin. Adrijana died in Sarajevo back in 1993. Your mind has suppressed it but you know that it's true. The girl you kidnapped is not your lover, she's not that girl you taught to speak English. She's not the girl who died at the torturing hands of a Serbian militia lunatic. She's not that beautiful girl that you fell in love with. She's Alicja Symanski, a girl who left Poland to work in Scotland and help her family, a young woman with her whole life in front of her. She's the girl you have to let go and live that life to the full. Give her the life that Adrijana never had.

You've got to give it up now, Colin and allow people who know what you've been through to help you."

I glanced from behind the wall. In the distance behind the farm buildings, I could see red and blue lights strobing in the rain. The sound of the vehicles' sirens drifted in on the wind.

Suddenly Rose stopped screaming and fell to his knees, clutching the gun like a precious jewel. He seemed to take a moment for contemplation then he raised the weapon slowly to his temple as I watched helplessly.

"Aw fuck, what have I done?" He held the pistol steadily, there was no trace of a shake. He looked to be sure of what he was about to do.

"I killed George, fuck I killed George. He only wanted to help and I killed him. Fuck, fuck, fuck." The visions of Bosnia had gone, and his mind had brought him back to a whole new host of horrors.

Steeling myself, I stood up. "Colin, listen, it's me, Craig. You can get help, Colin. There are professional people who understand what's happened to you. They understand the effect that it has had on you and they will be able to help you."

"No, I have to pay for what I've done. I killed George and Alicja's dead too. It's all my fault."

I climbed over the wall, courage coming from somewhere, I wasn't sure what the source was. No way would I ever face down anyone with a gun.

"No, Alicja's not dead. She's in the trees, I got her out before the fire took hold."

"No, you couldn't have. You're only saying that." He still held the gun to his own head, his tears masked by the rain water that covered his face.

"I did, I promise." I stepped towards him gingerly. Every fibre of my being screamed at me to go in the opposite direction but somehow I edged closer.

"If you put the gun down, I'll be able to show you. You can come with me and see that she's still alive."

His hand dipped a little but the sound of sirens grew stronger and he raised it again, pressing the barrel into his temple.

"Fuck, I'm sorry."

He pulled the trigger but instead of the sound

of a bullet penetrating his skull, there was a simple click. For a second it seemed as if every other sound in the universe disappeared, that dull click was the only noise I could hear.

The power returned to my legs in an instantaneous rush of adrenaline. I covered the short distance to him within a couple of seconds, throwing myself on top of him to prevent him reaching for more ammunition or another gun.

I prised the pistol from his grip but he put up little resistance, the fight had gone from him. I threw the gun as far as I could to my right, glad to be rid of the heated metal.

Having caught him, I had no idea what to do next. I needed to get to Alicja but there was no way to secure him. The decision was taken from me as three police cars screeched into the farm and up towards the blazing shed.

Within seconds there were six police officers pointing their guns at me. I stood up, my arms in the air.

"Armed police. Down on the ground, hands behind your head." I complied immediately and waited while two of the officers rushed towards us.

The cop patted me down and shouted, "Clear!" to his colleagues. The other officer did the same to Rose, lifting a box from Colin's pocket before putting him in handcuffs.

"We've got ammo here, Sarge."

The officer who had searched me told me to get up but took the precaution of keeping the gun firmly trained on me.

"Name?"

"Craig Campbell. I was the one that called."

"Who's he?" he indicated Rose with his head.

"Colin Rose. He owns this farm and another over the hill. Look, there's a young woman in a terrible mess in the wood back there. Can you get someone to go and help her?"

"Millar, Harper, check those woods."

"Be careful, she's very scared, guns might not be the best idea." I called after them. One of the officers took the other's gun, allowing him to conduct the search.

"What the fuck happened here?" The sergeant regarded me with cold blue eyes.

"It's kind of a long story but basically I think Colin's suffering from post traumatic stress. He kidnapped a girl believing her to be his long-dead girlfriend. He's also killed a man that worked for him, probably thinking he was going to harm Alicja, the girl in the woods. His name was George and his body was in the shed before it caught fire."

"Christ, there's going to be a shit load of paper work with this one."

I kept my own counsel on his comments.

There were further sirens as two fire engines and two ambulances made their way up the farm track.

As they arrived the two policemen returned from the woods, one of them carrying Alicja, who seemed to be unconscious again.

"Go down with my colleagues, get the paramedics to check you out, I'll deal with this Rose character," said the sergeant.

"I took a pistol from him and threw it over there." I indicated the general direction that I had propelled the gun.

"Right, we'll find it."

He left me and manhandled Colin Rose to his feet. Colin kept repeating how sorry he was and how it was all his fault.

I walked in a daze towards the banks of vehicles with their crowns of dancing light.

A paramedic stepped out from the crowd.

"Come on, we'll get you checked out." She guided me to one of the ambulances while Alicja was taken into the other one. Rose was placed in a police car.

One group of firefighters was putting out a small fire in the yard while the rest went to tackle the main blaze.

I had some minor cuts on my face from the bits of stone that had hit me but other than that I was fine. Despite my reassurances the paramedic insisted on giving me a full check. As she ran her various tests, the crowd scene was expanded further when two unmarked cars pulled into the busy farmyard. Four detectives joined the milling crowd of now redundant armed officers and the paramedics who were on standby for the still busy fire crew.

The rain had stopped, the storm having rolled on, oblivious to the drama that had played out under its darkened cloak.

Detective Sergeant Knowles appeared behind the paramedic, waiting patiently until she had given me the all clear.

"Mr Campbell, it seems you can't help finding yourself at the centre of a drama." He wore a stern look but his tone was sympathetic.

I must have looked sheepish as I replied, "Sorry about that."

"What's the story then?"

I gave him a brief sketch of the picture of despair I had uncovered. He nodded every now and again but left me to tell him what I knew.

"OK. You'll need to come to the station with us and give a full statement."

"I will do. I'll follow you down on the bike when you're ready."

One of the armed officers close by overheard me. "I don't think you will, sir." He gestured behind one of the cars.

I walked around to see my beloved Ducati covered in fire fighter's foam. It had caught fire after Rose had shot it before coming up to the shed.

"Shit."

DS Knowles stood beside me and laughed. "Oh

well, you won't be going anywhere on that again."

The detectives spent some time talking to the armed officers who were first on the scene. When he was finished with them Knowles spoke to me. "We were lucky those guys were nearby. They had been on a training course at the Fairmont Hotel. How to deal with the mental anguish of shooting a scumbag or some other pish."

Two of the other detectives set off to follow Alicja's ambulance to the hospital, hoping to get her statement as soon as possible. I imagined her tale would be as horrific to hear as it would be distressing for her to tell.

I watched as Rose was driven away by two of the armed PCs, staring off into the distance with a vacant look on his face. Then it was my turn to sit in the back of a car.

"DS Knowles, can we stop at the Rose farm, please? Rose's father needs to know what's happened and I need to speak to Danielus."

"OK, we'll speak to the father. I wouldn't normally bother but I think the man needs to know what his son has done, even if it's not all the guy's fault."

"Thanks."

After only a couple of minutes we were pulling into the courtyard of the Rose farm. The two detectives walked to the farmhouse while I made my way to Danielus' caravan.

He opened the door, looking as if I had woken

him up.

"Craig, what happened to you? Do you have news?"

"Yes, can we go in?"

"Will I get Stefania?"

"Yes, good idea."

I sat in the living area while Danielus went for Stefania. The shock seemed to have set in and I began to tremble. I did what I could to calm the tremors before they stepped into the caravan.

When they were both seated I began to tell them the story. "I found Alicja and she's alive."

They both reacted by making the sign of the cross. Tears of joy tumbled from their faces.

"She was abducted by Colin Rose. He has been suffering from post traumatic stress, I think since he came out of the army. A girlfriend of his was killed in a horrific way in the Balkans conflict. His mind was very disturbed when he kidnapped Alicja, he thought she was Adrijana, the girl who was killed. She's been pretty badly treated but I think she will be OK."

"How terrible." Danielus' face emphasised his shock.

"I'm afraid I also have some very bad news. Rose killed George with a shotgun. I think George must have discovered what was going on and tried to help Alicja."

Stefania's hands went to her mouth and her tears of joy turned to sorrow.

"This is terrible for the family of George. How will they live without their father?" It was Danielus who asked the question but I had no answers to offer.

"I'm sorry to be the one to tell you this. Will you contact Alicja's family and let them know she is safe?"

"Yes." Stefania nodded but the shock of the news about George had taken a toll.

Danielus thanked me and, my solemn duty completed, I said goodbye to them both.

When I got back to the car, both of the detectives were waiting for me.

"How did it go?" DS Knowles asked as I got into the back seat.

"Elation and sadness. You?"

"Just sadness. Mr Rose said he thought something wasn't right with Colin but he didn't know what. He's devastated."

We drove back to St Andrews in silence. I remembered Mrs Rose talking about a new girlfriend. I thought she had been talking about her husband. I presumed that it was a symptom of her condition but maybe she had been trying to tell me about Colin. It was the one clue that might have saved George's life and I cursed myself for missing it.

I felt sorry for Mr Rose, whose life had become even worse thanks to the actions of his disturbed son.

*

It was nearly nine before I sat down to a much-needed sandwich and a cup of brown slop masquerading as coffee. I sat in one of the interview rooms of St Andrews police station, going over my statement, ensuring that I hadn't missed anything.

DS Knowles was joined by DC Peters, the woman I had met briefly the previous day outside Michaels' house. So much had happened in such a short space of time. They questioned me repeatedly, making sure that they understood all that had happened.

"You rode your luck Mr Campbell, I hope you realise it," Peters said after I signed the formal statement.

"A little, yes. I couldn't phone you guys until I knew where she was, there was nothing I could tell you. When I did find her I had hoped to get her to safety without Rose appearing. How is Alicja, have you heard?"

Knowles answered, "She's been conscious but the doctors have sedated her to give her body a chance to recover. We'll have an officer with her until she's able to talk."

"What about Rose?"

"He's been talking. He hasn't asked for a lawyer. He confessed to the abduction of the girl and the murder of George Agyeman."

"What will happen to him?"

"We'll get a psychologist to talk to him in the morning. Everything you've told us points to him suffering from kind of PTS but the expert will get to the bottom of it. You never know, it could be an act, but I don't think so. He certainly went through some shit."

"What about Michaels?"

"Ah, now there's a real scumbag. Clammed up tighter than a duck's arse in a typhoon now that he's spoken to his lawyer, he's said nothing about anything since his brief arrived. We're still waiting for the DNA tests on the blood but if they're positive we should have enough, especially as we have the CCTV pictures of him picking her up that Saturday."

"Do you need anything else from me?"

"No, if we think of anything, we've got your number."

"I better organise a lift, I'll catch you later."

"Cheers, Craig."

I walked out into North Street and dialled Carol's mobile. The sound of her voice was enough to soothe away the aches, pains and anxiety of the day. The language she used when I told her about the bike was not what you would expect from a lady and it got even worse when I gave her the brief details of what else had happened. She agreed to come and get me.

I walked back to the Criterion to tell Bennett the sorry tale but he had already left. He would know soon enough.

On the journey from St Andrews to Cupar I filled in some of the details for Carol. In return she told me of her day with my Mum. They had spoken to the mortuary, who couldn't be sure if the baby, a little girl, was murdered. They reckoned she was only a few days old at most when she died.

When we arrived in Arbroath my mother shouted at me for a full ten minutes. I tried to tell her that none of it was my fault and that what happened couldn't have been anticipated but it was like trying to catch a gale with a kid's toy windmill.

She did brighten when I told her about the bike, but that was my only relief from the onslaught.

EPILOGUE

Two weeks later I stood over a tiny grave in a cemetery in Arbroath, as a Church Of Scotland minister committed the baby's body to the ground. My mother had named her Isabel in honour of the baby's mum.

The sun shone brightly over the group of strangers who had come to bury a girl who had died fifty years before. Carol stood beside me, with Mum and a couple of her neighbours on the opposite side. The minister, a Mrs Terrence, recited the words of religious service that I felt were always a little impersonal. She did at least have the excuse that no one knew very much about the tiny mite whose life we were commemorating.

When the short service was over we walked back to Mum's house. She had organised a small lunch of tea and sandwiches. The women chatted about Isabel and her tragic family. No one would ever be sure whether she was murdered or not. Mum had no luck tracing any of Isabel's relatives and had organised the funeral through the Co-operative Funeral Care, who did not charge for their services for the death of a child. Mum was defiant that the girl who had led a life that was too short would not be buried in an unmarked grave. A collection was raised in the neighbourhood to pay for her plot and a small stone to place on her grave.

When the guests had left, Mum asked if we were staying for dinner.

"Aye, Mum. We'll take you out for something," I suggested.

"That would be nice, son." The story of Isabel had a strange muting effect on her, she seemed to feel the pain as if she had known the baby and her family.

"Have you heard anything about the girl you found?" she asked.

"Yes, I spoke to Detective Knowles yesterday. Alicja was released from hospital and she's going home to Poland, at least for a wee while. I don't know if she'll be back."

"Why would she want come back after all she went through? The poor thing."

"The psychologists have said that Colin Rose is suffering from a very severe case of post-traumatic stress disorder. They reckon that he had suppressed completely what had happened to the woman in Bosnia. So much so, that it caused some kind of schism in his mind. One half of him wanted Alicja to look like how Adrijana looked the last time he saw her, to make her truly Adrijana. The other half wanted to protect her."

"Does that mean he was schizophrenic?"

"No, it's more like his memory was lost in time, flipping between Bosnia seventeen years ago and now. It's one of the typical symptoms of PTSD, he just had it worse than most."

"What'll happen to him?"

"DS Knowles wasn't sure. Rose will need treatment but he did murder George and that is a bit more difficult to explain away as part of his illness."

"It's such a mess. That poor lad's family back in Africa, Alicja, her family." She sighed.

"Don't forget Rose's parents. They've become victims of this as well."

"I suppose so. What about the lad that hired you, how's he after all this?"

"He's sad that Alicja's gone but he has met a guy and that seems to have given him something positive to help him cope."

"Good for him." She said it with little enthusiasm and for the first time I thought she looked old. I couldn't put my finger on it but something of her had diminished in the last couple of weeks.

Carol tried to lighten the mood. "Where we going to go for some food, then?"

"I fancy a proper Arbroath smokie, what d'you think, Mum?"

She seemed to brighten a little. "That sounds grand. I'll go and change, put my face on and we'll be off."

Twenty minutes later we were walking towards the restaurant, the two most important women in my life on either arm. I was ready to savour life again in the form of a good old Arbroath smoked haddock.

THE END

About The Author

Sinclair Macleod was born and raised in Glasgow. He worked in the railway industry for 23 years, the majority of which were in IT.

A lifelong love of mystery novels, including the classic American detectives of Hammett, Chandler and Ross Macdonald, inspired him to write his first novel, The Reluctant Detective. The Good Girl is the second novel featuring Craig Campbell.

Sinclair lives in Bishopbriggs, just outside his native city with his wife, Kim and daughter, Kirsten.

For more information go to
www.reluctantdetective.com

Also Available by Sinclair Macleod

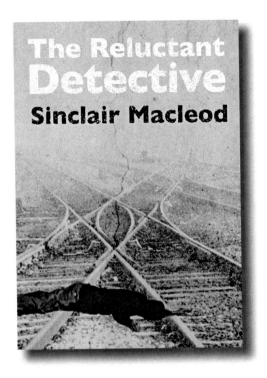

"I want you to find who killed my son."

Craig Campbell's quiet life as an insurance investigator is turned upside down when Ann Kilpatrick hires him to find her son's killer. He reluctantly agrees but doesn't believe he can really help.

Before long he is plunged into a world of corruption, deceit and greed. His journey takes him from the underbelly of Glaswegian society to the rural idyll of a millionaire's mansion.

Along the way, a death close to home ensures that he has a personal reason to face the dangers and bring the murderer to justice.

Available in paperback and for the iPad and Kindle

Lightning Source UK Ltd.
Milton Keynes UK
UKOW032057071111

181629UK00002B/44/P